James Gardner Sanderson

Cornell Stories

James Gardner Sanderson

Cornell Stories

ISBN/EAN: 9783744748049

Printed in Europe, USA, Canada, Australia, Japan

Cover: Foto ©Andreas Hilbeck / pixelio.de

More available books at **www.hansebooks.com**

CORNELL STORIES

BY

JAMES GARDNER SANDERSON

NEW YORK
CHARLES SCRIBNER'S SONS
1898

To B. D. T.

Contents

THE WOOING OF MELVILLE R. CORYDON

1

Cornell Stories

❧

THE WOOING OF MELVILLE R. CORYDON

J. E. Thorpe, R. T.,
  Rho Tau Lodge, Ithaca, N. Y.

New York, June 14, 189-.

DEAR JIMMY, — Don't faint with the sudden shock of receiving a letter from me. The daring · with which I bound thusly into the arena, as a competitor in the art of polite letter-writing, explains itself when I tell you of a wonderful fish I have been trying to land for you all summer. He is a young and good-looking fish who plays baseball and football, being better at the latter than the former, I believe, and does stunts on a couple of musical instruments also. His name is Melville R. Corydon, and his father is R. F. Corydon, one of our leading bankers here, and very prominent, socially.

3

Young Corydon is very popular with his crowd here, and although I have not been able to see much of him I have improved the opportunities which have chanced my way, and have thrown R. T. into him in chunks as large as your head, so that I believe his one desire in life is to join the society that turns out hot men — such as you and I, for instance.

I do not believe the fellows would make the least mistake in taking the boy, as he has the right kind of stuff in him, and ought to make a star. You want to get after him hard, I think; but I do not anticipate much trouble if you work him in the right way. Any influence I may be able to wield down here is, of course, at your service.

Corydon arrives on the noon train to-morrow — D. L. & W. Some of you ought to go up to the switch. Love to all the boys.

Yours in R. T.,

MYRON J. PRITCHARD.

Why the deuce don't some of you fellows write occasionally?

FORTUNATUS CONSTANTINE WORKMAN,
  BETA CHI HOUSE, ITHACA, N. Y.

JERSEY CITY, June 14, 189–.

MY DEAR SON, — I enclose your June draft. This will be all I shall send for Senior week, as both your mother and I feel that you are spending more than is necessary this term. At all events, you are spending more than I ever dreamed of having when I was your age; and while I agree with you, to some extent, when you say "times have changed, and are continually changing," I would suggest that when you run short you draw on that "continual change" instead of upon me. I shall answer no further letters in which you ask for more.

Why do you need a hat box? When I was a boy we *wore* our silk hats. I hardly see the advantage of buying an eight-dollar hat and carrying it around in a box. However, I can talk with you about that later.

I hope you have succeeded in your examinations this term. I do not like the thought of a son of mine being conditioned. Acknowledge draft at once.　　Aff'tly,　　FATHER.

P. S.   I understand that young Corydon, the son of R. E. Corydon who is part of the Co. in R. F. Corydon and Co., bankers, of New York, is going to take his entrance examinations for Cornell, in Ithaca, to-morrow.   Your mother and I both think it would be a nice thing for you to look him up and pay him some little attention for the sake of the friendship between the families.   He seems like a nice boy, and is very quiet, and a hard worker.   He is president of our Christian Endeavor Society, and has recently been helping Mr. Lee, who, you will remember, is at present superintendent of our Sunday-school.   F.

WM. A. HILDRETH,
    CHI DELTA SIGMA HOUSE,
        CORNELL UNIVERSITY, ITHACA, N. Y.

Corydon, son of R. A. Corydon, of R. F. Corydon & Co., arrives on noon train to-morrow.   Good fellow, but quite sporty.   Rush hard.   Have written.

PIKE.

On a certain sunshiny morning in June the gray-coated postman, looking not unlike a Roman charioteer in civilized garb, as he stood in the back of his two-wheeled delivery wagon, left these two letters at their proper destinations. Five minutes later a snub-nosed boy, wearing the red-corded cap of the Western Union, shuffled across the piazza of another fraternity house, pointed with a smudgy finger to a certain line in his yellow-leafed booklet, received his signature, and shuffled away.

Among the Greek letter societies at Cornell, Rho Tau, Beta Chi, and Chi Delta Sigma stood high among the leaders. As the last roster included about thirty-one societies, the positions of the big three were most enviable. Their lists invariably contained the names of men most prominent in university affairs; and the far-spread fame of these names, coupled with the initials of their society, brought many entering freshmen and many more soon-to-be-entering sub-freshmen to college with quickened heart-beats and a deep, unspoken determination to join (if they were lucky enough to be asked) the society whose pin X, the football captain, wore, or the one to which Y, the funny man on the Glee Club, belonged, or that of which Z, who made Phi Beta Kappa, was a member. The tacit acknowledgment by the university at large of the big threes' superiority increased their strength, and year after year, with the going of seniors, the making of alumni, and the coming of freshmen, they grew in power, until now, between them and the others, there was little rivalry in the matters of rushing.

This was the relation in which three stood to twenty-eight. Unfortunately this power-born peace did not extend to the big threes' relations with each other. Among themselves the rivalry was intense. One year the Rho Taus would succeed in winning a freshman who had been offered an invitation to each of the other two. The next year, or, possibly, during the same season, the Beta Chis would bid and pledge a man in the very teeth of the fiercest rushing of Rho Tau and Chi Delta Sigma.

The next desirable man might fall under the fascinations of the Chi Delts, and so the see-saw went. Now one would triumph, now another, and many a freshman who had been dined, theatred, driven, and generally made to feel that each crowd was the finest set of fellows ever born, and he the finest of them all, has sat down after it was all over, and his choice was made, and wondered why he was being sworn at and ordered about with so much less consideration than he had been led to believe he deserved.

Competition, in rushing, almost assumes the ear-marks of a science when three strong societies are in the field. Attention is given to even the minutest details. If a freshman who is being rushed is an athlete, athletics are the topic, and 'varsity sweaters are thrown carelessly around the house. If the man is of a religious turn of mind, hymns are played and "cussing" suppressed. If he leans toward beer and chorus-girls, beer and chorus-girls are put before him. His slightest wish and inclination is consulted

9

—until he is pledged. He is met by a representative of each society, invited to their houses, and, in the guise of an honored guest, given a chance to inspect and be inspected. If a society decides favorably, no pains are spared to impress him with the superiority of their particular men and their particular society. In due time he receives a bid, which is college slang for an offer of election. The complications arising when three or four men are being rushed by as many societies are often intricate and require the exercise of unlimited tact and diplomacy.

Therefore it fell out on this sunny summer morning that excitement reigned supreme in the houses of Rho Tau, Beta Chi, and Chi Delta Sigma.

As J. E. Thorpe read his mail his eyes danced; and, calling his senior classmates together, he read them the letter.

"See here, fellows," said he, "from what Pritchard says, we want that man."

"Pity he didn't tell us before," said Fair-

10

banks. "We could have done some preliminary work."

"I rather guess we don't need it," replied Thorpe. "He says the boy has a strong leaning our way already."

"We need another athlete and musician, if he is a good fellow," chimed in Stark. "Jimmy, hadn't you and Torresdale better go up to the switch to-morrow? It's not likely if the man is such a ' star ' that the Chi Delts or Beta Chis don't know about his coming. If they do, they will be there also. We don't want to take chances with those people."

"Right, O Molly," answered Thorpe. "Bobby, we'll be there."

"We'll show him our football man, eh, Jimmy?" crooned Blake, idly flattening Torresdale's nose with his tennis racket as he lay sprawling on the divan.

Torresdale rose in his might and sat heavily on his tormentor. Then he said, "*And* the Glue Club man. Sing, Blakey. Sing, or I'll yank — !"

"Ow-wow-iyi — oh! Hully Gee, you fat lobster! Lemme go!" cried Blake, clutching wildly at his hair and scrambling to his feet.

"*And* the Glue Club man," repeated Torresdale, with a satisfied sigh, as he fell back once more to cushioned ease.

"He is musical," said Stark. "Remember that, fellows; and — perhaps Blake had better not sing while he is in the house." ·

"We'll take him to call on the three prettiest girls in town," suggested Blake, ignoring Stark's last remark.

"Well, anyway we'll rush him," said Thorpe, decisively. "We'll rush him hard. Therefore it behooves all you fellows to be here when Bobby and I bring him up. Somebody tell the freshmen. Let's eat."

. . . .

"Um-huh," said Puggy Workman from his chair by the window, as he unfolded his father's letter. "Same thing. I wonder if I really *am* spending too much. Hat box, — used to wear his hat, too. Dear, dear! I suppose he did.

Wore a frock with red morocco slippers and a polo cap, too, I dare say. Ah, well — He's the best father I ever had. Um — um — um — Hello! — say, fellows, listen to this," and Puggy read aloud the last few lines of his letter. The crowd around the table looked interested.

"Do you know him?" asked Hollister, rather dubiously.

"No," replied Puggy, "I don't. You see, I have lived in New York with my uncle most of my life, and don't know very many Jersey City people. But I know his rep. at home, and I know his mother. He is mighty well thought of, and is as bright as a whip."

"Has he a he-mother?" queried Wilbur, with polite surprise.

"Do you know whether he is *obtrusively* good, Puggy?" asked Ferris. "That letter seems to convey that impression. If he is, Hollister's nervous system will simply be ruined, you know."

"Oh, come inside, fellows," said Puggy,

tersely. "What are we going to do? Shall we look at him or let him slide? It seems to me that we'd better look him up, at least. A good man won't hurt us. Moreover," and Puggy pointed an emphatic forefinger at the offending Wilbur, who was seated on the table, nursing his knee, "the Chi Delts and the Rho Taus will be after him, for they both have alumni in Jersey City. If the Chi Delts can stand any one who is good — that is, *pious* you know, — there will be a hot rush between them. Now what? Shall we give them a whirl or not? We shall have to be careful at first, you know, if we do. No cussing, or anything like that, until we know how he takes such things."

"We might look at him, just to show our friends who we are," suggested Hollister. "But if we touch it, we don't want any half-way business. It must be good, hard rushing, or nothing. What do you fellows say?"

"We ought to have a man in Jersey City," said Ferris. "The Rhos and the Chi Delts both have a pull there through their alumni. I say

14

let's rush him. Nobody is going to make us take him if he is on the reform platform."

"Well, gentlemen, step up, step up," called Puggy. "Who will go up to the switch with me to-morrow?"

Hollister volunteered, and Wilbur offered to teach the rest hymns while they were waiting. He said he knew some excellent hymns which sounded immense played in rag time.

.   .   .   .

"Hi, there, you oldest senior in the bunch," drawled Punk Hildreth, as he strolled into Fordyce's room, where the latter sat wrestling with his long overdue thesis. "Call out your dogs of war. Turn loose thy flowing locks, and let thy face, now sicklied o'er with the pale cast of thought, brighten with the glow of battle."

"What's the matter now?" asked Fordyce, pushing back the papers before him with a sigh of relief, and looking up at Hildreth with a smile.

"Jack, you have an extremely sicklied-o'er face to-day," replied his friend, looking at him critically. "I presume that, laboring under the disadvantages that such a face naturally —"

"Is that all you disturbed me for?" asked Fordyce, reaching for a shoe.

"Let me think," said Punk, edging in front of the mirror. "No, it was n't — really. I 've a telegram for you. But throw your old shoe if you want to."

"Let 's look."

Hildreth threw the despatch into his lap.

Fordyce read it and grinned. "Old Pikey, eh? — 'Good fellow, but quite sporty.' We 'll look him up, and treat him accordingly. Like Pikey, was n't it, to run us against a proposition of that sort?"

"He says, 'Have written,'" said Hildreth, sitting carelessly on the title-page of the thesis. "That means that he intends specifying the particular way in which Mr. Corydon likes his alcohol prepared."

"We can't stand a man who sets too hot a pace," said Fordyce, biting his pen meditatively.

"He 'll run with the sporty freshman."

"Or you."

"Humph!"

"Will you go up to the switch with me to-morrow?"

"Noon train?" asked Hildreth.

"Yes."

"Yes."

"As you go out put a notice in the hall so the fellows will know he is coming," observed Fordyce, rolling his classmate off his thesis, and gathering the loose sheets together.

Hildreth mussed his hair, and ran to the door. He stood on the sill with one arm raised as a shield to prospective shoes, and said, plaintively, —

"Jack, that telegram came collect. It's really a rushing expense, you know — ?"

Biff! went the shoe against the door-jamb. Punk dodged and walked away with a quiet sigh.

. . . .

The three-car train came panting and puffing up the steep grade of the second switch.

It was four days before the beginning of Senior week, too soon for the crowd to be either coming or going. One or two travelling men, a couple of farmers' wives, three or four Ithaca business-men, and three sub-freshmen, each of whom was wondering to what class at Cornell the others belonged, were scattered along the seats of the second car.

The old conductor, on the lookout for fares from Caroline, came walking through from the smoker. The conductor of the noon train of that particular run has accumulated the privileges of seventeen years' steady work, and had seen the waking and growth of class after class, and the coming of many vacations. He paused before one of the sub-freshmen as one who has a right.

"Examinations?" he asked, with a kindly smile.

The sub-freshman hesitated for the fraction of a second. He wanted to lie and indignantly deny his newness, but a glance at the old conductor's face changed his mind.

"Yes," he said.

"You'll see the university buildings in half a minute more," said the conductor, and passed on through the train.

The boy flattened his face against the window-pane. As the train rolled out from between two hills he saw a farmhouse, then a cluster of smaller houses, and then, without a note of warning, the cars jerked around a curve, and across the valley the grandeur and beauty of the campus lay before him. For a moment he held his breath. He was conscious of a queer little thrill as the curtain thus rose on the first scene in his college life. He had never even seen a picture of the campus, and he looked out eagerly at the buildings around which and between whose walls there lay such a wealth of sweet, untasted mystery. He looked down at the town clinging to the hillside and straggling over the lowlands. He looked at the lake winding its rippling bends and turnings into the dimness of the hazy forest banks, and then he looked at all three, and sighed contentedly.

19

Just then the break-shoes squeaked and screeched, the exhaust-pipes whistled, and the train came to a stop. The car door opened, and two students entered quickly. The sub looked up, and his heart leaped within him, for he had noticed that both wore sweaters with large white C's decorating the breasts, and that on the red, short-visored cap of one there appeared the cabalistic letters C.U.B.B.C. worked into a monogram. From the sweater and the cap he judged them, correctly, 'varsity men, and he watched them out of the corners of his eyes.

He tried to look as if he were only going to Ithaca to visit friends, and succeeded in stamping himself so unmistakably sub that Torresdale and Thorpe nudged each other, and bore quickly down upon him. The sub saw them looking at him, and looked out of the window. His ideas of hazing were vague, but he had heard that the slightest freshness was fatal, and not knowing whether it was fresh to stare, awe-struck, at a 'varsity man, he looked out of the window. The men stopped in front of him.

20

"I beg your pardon," began Thorpe, pleasantly, "but is your name Corydon?"

The boy turned suddenly, "I — I beg your
pardon?" said he.

"Is your name Corydon?" repeated Thorpe.

"Yes," said the sub, nervously.

"My name's Thorpe — Jim Thorpe. Myron
Pritchard wrote me you were coming to-day,
and asked me to put you on to the ropes a bit.
It's rather hard for a new man at first, you
know, unless he knows some one," and Mr.
Thorpe smiled sympathetically.

"Oh! — oh, yes," said Corydon, taking the
offered hand. "Mr. Pritchard has spoken of
you to me very often. You're a — a — you
belong to his society, don't you?"

"Yes, I'm a Rho Tau," answered Thorpe,
smiling. "I don't blame you for not remem-
bering; there are so many of them, you know.
Oh, by the way — I want you to know the captain of our next year's football team. You
play, I understand."

Corydon blushed as Torresdale shook hands,

and said, in his big voice, "I heard something of your playing while you were at St. Paul's, Corydon. You must be sure and try for the team next fall. I'll be very glad to give you any points I can, if you care for them."

"Maybe you can dine with us to-night," Thorpe broke in before Corydon could stammer his thanks. "Torry, here, is a Rho Tau, too, you know, and you fellows can gas football to your hearts' content."

"Why — why, thank you," said Corydon, rather dazed at this suddenness; "I think I'd better — "

"I'll tell you," interrupted Torresdale, "you come with us, and we'll fix you out at your hotel. Then come up to dine and spend the evening. How does that strike you?" and Torresdale laid his hand familiarly on the sub's shoulder.

"I should like it very much," said the sub, "only I don't want to bother you fellows."

"Oh, nonsense," said Thorpe, laughing.

"We'll tell you when we are being bothered. Don't worry."

Torresdale echoed the laugh, and sat down beside him, for he had seen two hostile figures in the distance. Thorpe had just time to slide into the seat ahead as the door opened and Hollister and Puggy Workman entered.

Puggy came down the aisle, looking sharply from side to side. When they reached the first sub-freshman he bent over and asked him a question. He shook his head and they walked on. The second was still looking out of the window at the campus when Hollister tapped him on the shoulder. Torresdale and Thorpe chuckled as they left him and stood looking hopelessly around the car. Suddenly Puggy caught sight of the strange face wedged in between the big guard and the window, and, pulling himself together, walked briskly toward them, closely followed by Hollister.

"Hello, Jimmy! How are you, Torresdale?" he said, with his blandest smile, and, without giving the two men a chance to recover from their astonishment at the boldness of this move, dropped into the vacant seat behind them, and, leaning over, said in a confidential tone to the sub, —

"Isn't your name Corydon?"

The sub looked up, startled, at this second self-introduced young man. He had thought that he was unknown up here, but already, before he was off the train, here were four fellows who evidently knew who he was. The first instance he could understand; but what did this second mean? He turned with an odd look at Torresdale, sitting grimly at his side, and answered.

"I thought so," said Puggy. "I used to live in your town. My father does now. You know him, I think — Workman?"

The sub's face lighted up.

"Yes, I know him," he said. "I am very glad to meet you, Mr. Workman. I had the pleasure of knowing your sister quite well."

"Is that so," said Puggy, heartily. "I am glad to hear it. How is she?"

He knew there was something wrong, as he was an only child, but he preferred to defer all explanations.

"Why — er — " said Corydon, growing rather red, "she died last summer."

"Oh! that one," said Puggy, taken aback somewhat. "Yes, she did. That's so — it was very sad, you know. Poor thing!"

The sub looked rather astonished. "Had you two sisters?" he asked.

"Yes, indeed," replied Puggy, unblushingly. "One you never met. I — but I beg your pardon, Hollister, old man. Let me present Mr. Corydon."

"Mr. Corydon, I am very glad to meet you. Glad to see you have picked out the proper college," said Hollister, shaking hands vigorously. "Workman told me you were coming, and we thought we would drop down and meet you, just to see if we could do anything, you know. Stranger, you know. Can't you come and let us look up a room for you this afternoon?"

"Thank you, — thank you very much," said the sub; "but I 've accepted Mr. Thorpe's offer for this afternoon. He — "

"Come and dine with us then," suggested Puggy.

"Why — I 've promised Mr. Torresdale," said Corydon, with an embarrassed laugh. The situation was a trifle strained.

"Drop in and see us to-night," hazarded Hollister. "We 'd like to have you meet the men in our fraternity. Just ask for either Workman or me. Torresdale will show you where our house is, I am sure."

"Thank you," said Corydon. "I think I can do that all right. It 's awfully nice of you fellows to trouble yourselves this way."

"Not at all," said Workman. "We'll all be mighty glad to see you. Nine? Yes. Good-bye," and the two fellows rose, shook hands, and vanished.

Corydon and his two pilots, one on either side, safely navigated the shoals of State Street, and steered to the dingy haven of so many lost subs, — the Ithaca Hotel. As they entered the office two very red-faced students, with wilted collars and streaming faces, moved aside from the desk with a greeting to Thorpe and Torresdale. Fordyce and Hildreth had evidently missed the train.

As Corydon thrust the pen back into the bowl of shot after registering, Fordyce stepped up to obtain a match for some prospective pipe. Glancing at the book, he took the match, walked back to his companion, and nodded. Hildreth immediately pushed himself between Torresdale and Thorpe with a polite "Pardon me," and, addressing the oily looking clerk, said, "Pat, Charlie Pike wired me yesterday that a friend of his named Corydon, whom he wanted me to meet, was coming in to-day. Seen anything of him?"

Corydon looked up startled. This was new to him. After his two experiences in the train he had rather expected every two men he saw together to shake his hand and ask him to dinner, and it had finally dawned upon him that he was being rushed; but he was not used to this new style of procedure. He cleared his throat and took a step forward.

"I — " he began.

"Corydon?" asked Hildreth, turning with a smile and outstretched hand and speaking rapidly. "Went down to meet you. Missed train. Hot, is n't it? My friend Mr. Fordyce, Mr. Corydon. Yes; oh, yes, we both know Thorpe and Torresdale, thank you. Hot, is n't it? Let 's all go get a mint-julep. There is a man in back there who really mixes a very superior article. Oh, yes, you do. What? Oh, come along. A friend of Pike's, and don't — Oh, that 's very good — really, very good. Ha! ha! Torry, here, is a regular soak, are n't you, Torry? Come on, Thorpe."

Torresdale and Thorpe looked dazed. Had Hildreth been affected by the heat? Hildreth, of all men mild, to ask a sub-freshman to drink in almost the first words he spoke! There was something wrong somewhere; but Hildreth gathered them in, and pushed them all before him to the little rear room, where, at his command, the genial, white-coated George pounded mint and sliced pineapples industriously for a few moments. Then Hildreth threw a bill airily on the bar, and, raising his glass to Corydon, buried his nose in the fragrant leaves until nothing but the fragrant leaves remained. Thorpe and Torresdale, unable to resist, followed suit, and Corydon, smiling uncertainly, imitated them. Then, after a few moments of desultory conversation, Hildreth made Corydon promise to stop at the house and see him on his way down from examinations the next morning, and the two men disappeared.

"Punk," said Fordyce, meditatively, "I think you made a fool of yourself there. I don't believe that fellow's the sport that Pikey made him out to be. Did you notice that he left fully half of his drink?"

"No!" said Punk. "Let's go back. Well, maybe I did. *I* can't act like a sport. We'll see."

Torresdale, Thorpe, and Corydon went down

the hotel steps in search of lunch. The sub, who had recovered his self-possession, stared around curiously. This was the first time he had ever been in Ithaca; and the old New York town, born over a century ago, and almost undiscovered, until Ezra Cornell laid the first foundations of a great university upon the hill above its quiet streets, possessed for him the attraction of anticipation. The students strolling in twos and threes up and down State Street fascinated him. He longed for the fall that he might be among them, and he resolved to number among his first purchases a red sweater with a large collar and white lacings, and an amber-stemmed drop-pipe. Later he coveted one of the silk Cornell flags displayed in a certain shop-window further down the street. He looked eagerly, in passing, at the pictures of the campus in the corner book-store, and bowed tardily as his companions raised their gray felt slouches to the pretty girl who was talking to the senior partner in the firm. The very air of the street was intoxicating, with its subtle suggestions of fellowship; and when, after a block and a half, they turned into a student resort for lunch, and he heard the sound of a dozen voices singing to the accompaniment of pounding beer glasses, his heart gave a joyful leap, for all this and much more was the beginning of his college life.

As they entered, the men at the table yelled, "Yeea, Torry! Yeea, Thorpe!" and scraped their chairs and crowded to make room for them. But Torresdale shook his head and smiled, and led the way to a white-clothed table in a far corner of the room. Corydon was rather sorry. He would have liked it better nearer those fellows, he thought, but, of course, did not say anything, and sat down meekly in the chair which Thorpe politely pulled out for him.

"That's the upper-classman table," explained Thorpe. "Only upper-classmen are allowed to sit there."

"Oh," replied the sub, "I hope — I hope I did not keep you or Mr. Torresdale away from it."

"Oh, no," said Thorpe, carelessly. "We are there often enough, as it is."

"Too often," smiled Torresdale; and then he added, in a lower tone, "Some of those fellows are rather muckerish."

"Oh!" said the sub again. He did not exactly understand, but he was learning, and, for the present, was content merely to sit by the captain of the football team and the pitcher of the baseball team, and drink in their words.

His bosom swelled with pride. What would some of those St. Paul's fellows say if they could only see him now beside the mighty Torresdale, who was slated for guard of the All America team the year before? What if they should hear Thorpe calling him "old man," just as though he had known him all his life, — Thorpe, who pitched on the crack team of '9–! And what nice fellows they were! He had no idea they were both so nice. In fact, he had never thought of them as men, merely as athletes, when he read the papers. He wondered if he was behaving as he ought. He did not know just how he ought to act. He had never talked to any 'varsity men before, and he did not know just what to do or say, so he leaned back and listened to what Torresdale was saying.

"The fellows come down here and sing almost every Saturday night in term time," said Torresdale. "You'll learn to know this as Pat's, in time. There's Pat now — that well-fed looking personage talking to Jack Crawford. Crawford's that fellow at the end. He's on the Banjo Club."

"Is he — does he belong to your fraternity?"

"Well, not to any great extent," said Thorpe, contemptuously. "He —"

"Jim!" said Torresdale, sharply.

"Humph!" retorted Thorpe, lucidly.

"You see," explained Torresdale, "Crawford and Jimmy here don't love each other, for reasons which you may know some day. The Rho Taus, however, when entertaining a guest, make it an invariable rule not to speak badly of any man of another society. It don't look clean, you know."

"I see," said the sub, vaguely.

Thorpe gulped down a swallow of coffee, and looked forbidding, and, for a moment or two, the three were silent. The sub had just begun to wonder if he had made a break of any sort, when a tall young man, with thin ankles and an incipient mustache, both visible as he stood peering over the swinging half-doors leading to the main room, yelled, "Ay, there, Jimmy Thorpe!"

"Hello, Colonel!" cried Thorpe, forgetting all his wrath on the instant. "Come on in. There's a man you must meet, Corydon. One of our fellows, and a bully one, too. More fun!" said Thorpe, enthusiastically.

As Blake came down the room, the crowd at the upper-classman table yelled vociferously, and plucked at his coat to make him sit down with them. Blake drew back with an assumption of hauteur, and, pointing his finger at them in a mock gesture of scorn, said, slowly, and in a cracked voice, "Y-e worrrmss!" and escaped in a shower of crackers.

For some reason Corydon thought this remarkably funny, and he snorted aloud. Then he noticed that Thorpe and Torresdale were only smiling, and he choked down his mirth and blushed.

"We 're used to him," said Torresdale; "but he *is* funny."

"I think that was awfully funny," said Corydon.

"He could have been the funny man on the Glee Club," said Thorpe, in his ear, after he had shaken hands with this curious junior. "Gave it up for leadership of the Banjo Club."

The sub looked up with renewed interest, as Blake answered a question of Thorpe's in a way that set them all laughing. Surely he was meeting the most prominent men in college, — the captain of one team, the pitcher of another, and the leader of the Banjo Club! Who would come next, he wondered.

He was puzzled. Were all freshmen treated this way, or was this another phase of that

mysterious proceeding called rushing? It probably was, he said to himself, and yet even that
did not explain many things. For instance,
that round-faced fellow on the train, — why had
he seemed so embarrassed when he had spoken
of his sister? Then Hildreth at the hotel?
Who was Charlie Pike? He had never heard
of any one by the name of Pike. And how
queerly Hildreth had acted. And yet they all
seemed nice fellows.

His thoughts were interrupted by Blake, who
was telling about a Banjo Club rehearsal he had
just attended. He was lamenting the lack of
sufficient banjeaurines for the coming year.
Suddenly, as if struck by a new thought, he
turned to Corydon.

"Corydon, you play the banjeaurine, don't
you?" he said.

"A little," the sub admitted.

"Good! You will try for the clubs next
year, of course?"

"I — I don't believe I play well enough,"
stammered Corydon, taken by surprise.

"Oh, nonsense! You try, anyway. It's a good honor, you know."

"Yes, by all means try," chimed in Thorpe. "The Colonel will put you on to the ropes."

"Well," said Torresdale, heartily, "whatever else he may do, he is going to play football, and *that's* no lie. Let's go on up the hill."

The men rose. Thorpe wrote his name across the check in the face of the sub's protests, and threw it across the bar to Marnit, who bowed respectfully, and said, "All right, Mr. Thorpe." Then the four went out and waited for a car.

When they reached the house, Thorpe went around and gathered the men together. He brought them up one after another, and intro- duced them to Corydon. They all shook hands very cordially, and said they had heard of his football playing, and were glad he was coming to Cornell.

Now it is a hard thing to put a sub-freshman at his ease before a room full of college men whom he has just met, and at first Corydon felt a little out of his element. But when he found that one of the fellows knew two men with whom he had been camping the summer before, and that another had met his brother, who was a Yale man, at Bar Harbor, and that still another knew several girls he knew at Dobb's Ferry, his embarrassment proved short-lived.

As they fell to talking of each other's prep. schools and younger associations, always carefully avoiding ground which was unfamiliar to their guest, his reserve fell from him as a cloak. He laughed and joked with the men nearest him, and guyed back gayly at the freshman opposite, who was making fun of St. Paul's. He laughed, until his cheeks ached, at Blake's stories and imitations. He listened, with bated breath, to Torresdale's description of the last game against Princeton, and his eyes shone as he told how, with the ball in Princeton's hands on Cornell's one yard line, the Cornell line had held and thrown the Tigers back four times, and then had punted out of danger.

The Rho Taus had done as they wished. They had made their man act naturally, and be oblivious to their own inspection. This is the hardest thing to do in rushing a freshman. No man who was being rushed ever entered a fraternity house, and sat before the battery of sixteen or twenty pairs of eyes without feeling as though he were being criticised, and, feeling thus, they cannot act naturally. Unless they are themselves, it is very hard for the fraternity to decide upon them. Therefore the freshman must become so deeply interested as to lose sight of himself, and the fraternity, of course, must interest him. This serves a double purpose, for, being interested, the freshman, or sub, has a good time, and thus begins to like the crowd and the men in it.

When, finally, Thorpe rose, and asked Corydon if he would not like to look over the house, Corydon felt as though never in all his life had he come across such a uniformly congenial crowd of men. When, under Thorpe's guidance, he inspected the house from top to bottom, with the exception of one room, past the iron-barred, oaken door of which Thorpe led him with an air which forbade questions, he was charmed. The cozy studies and bedrooms, the large dining-room, and the library and reception-rooms met with his undisguised approval. Life in such a house, and with such fellows, seemed idyllic, and he breathed a prayer to fate that he might not be weighed and found wanting.

After he had seen the house, a senior and a freshman took him up the campus, and he was shown the different halls and buildings in which he, as a freshman, would work in the fall. On their way back, the senior pointed out to him the library lecture-room where he was to take his English examination on the following morning.

After dinner Blake went to the piano, and every one stood up and put his arm around every one else's neck and sang. For the greater part they sang Rho Tau songs, and Corydon noticed that as they came to the choruses every man tightened his hold on his neighbor's shoulders, and sang as though his whole heart were

in the music and words. He had time for only
a very little wonder; for, changing, Blake broke
into Alma Mater, and Torresdale beckoned to
him to come up and sing with them. Now very
few men who are entering Cornell, and none
who are once in college, hear Alma Mater for
the first time without feeling their pulses bound
and their hearts beat; and this particular sub
was no exception. As the harmony rang through
the room, with Blake's full, sweet tenor soaring
above all, Corydon stood and listened. When
it was ended, he sighed unconsciously, and, grip-
ping Torresdale's arm, said, huskily, —

"By George, Mr. Torresdale, I'm glad I am
coming here to college."

Torresdale smiled back understandingly. He
had heard it for the first time three years
ago.

The songs went on; and Corydon, joining in
those he knew, and thinking and listening during those he had not heard, let the time slip by
in simple happiness. When the booming of
the library clock woke him to the remembrance

of his engagement with Hollister, he rose, and Blake stopped playing.

"You're not going?" he said, rising.

"I'm afraid I shall have to," replied the sub, reluctantly. "I promised Mr. Hollister that I would call on him for a short time this evening."

"But it's early yet."

"I know, but I promised. It's not because I care so much about it."

"Don't keep him if he has a date, Colonel," said Thorpe; and then, as an afterthought, "why can't you come back here afterwards? We are going to have a rarebit to-night, and we'd like to have you."

"Jove! but you've a head, Jimmy," said Torresdale. "That's the idea."

"Good! Do that. Any time. Just ring. Break away as soon as you can," chorused the rest; and Corydon, hesitating, had promised almost before he knew it.

They all went out on the steps with him as Torresdale pointed out the Beta Chi house.

"Now be back as soon as you can, old man,"

he said; and the sub promised again, and disappeared into the darkness.

The men filed back into the house. Thorpe stood with his back against the door, and addressed the crowd.

"Fellows," he said, "that was the best piece of rushing we've done since Willy died. I am proud of you. Now I suppose we have got to make a rarebit. Some of you freshmen go hunt for that chafing-dish."

. . . .

Corydon entered the Beta Chi house. His head was awhirl with his new experiences, and he pinched himself just to make sure that he was the same lowly person who had left New York in fear and trembling the night before. Workman and Hollister received him with open arms, and piloted him into the reception-room. Excusing themselves, they left him for a moment; and Corydon said to himself, "Now there will be sixteen new men who will come pouring into this room in three minutes. I shall have to shake hands with them all, and then they will ask questions. Humph!" from which it will be seen that Corydon was still learning.

He had hardly time to look around and decide that the Rho Tau reception-room was prettier, before they all came trooping in. Corydon stood up by Hollister's side. He felt like the President of the United States, as one man after another advanced, grasped his hand, and uttered a few words of welcome; but he was sincerely thankful when it was over and he could sit down. He found a seat vacant, of course by the merest chance, between the stroke of the 'varsity crew and the editor-in-chief of the last *Cornellian*. They were both well-dressed, jovial fellows; but somehow there was a suspicion of artificiality in their actions, and an excess of interest apparent in their manner when Corydon spoke. Corydon noticed this, and, consequently, did not feel at ease. Hence the crew man and the *Cornellian* editor did not exert the influence or inspire the awe that was hoped.

In another way, too, Corydon saw a difference in his treatment. The Rho Taus had talked of those things which interested him,—the college life, the teams, the crew, and a little of those studies which he hoped to take up in the fall. The Beta Chis paid not one whit of attention to any of these things but study. Studies and church seemed to be their only joys. Several men asked Corydon if he were going to join the Y.M.C.A. The crew man offered to introduce him to the president of the association; and when Corydon said that he guessed he would wait until fall, the *Cornellian* editor asked him if he would not like to have him speak to the aforesaid president, and tell him that Corydon was coming, and would be glad to help in prayer-meeting. The sub looked rather embarrassed, and repeated that he guessed he would wait until fall. Then Puggy Workman, finding out that he was an Episcopalian, asked him if he would not like to take a class in the Sunday-school of the church down town when he came to college. Corydon guessed again, and then Hollister offered to take him down to service on the following Sunday.

Try as the sub might, by his questions concerning college affairs and fraternity life, he could not hold them back. It was the church, the church, and always the church.

It was too much. From church they went to study again, and four or five formed a group around Corydon, and fell into a warm discussion as to the nature of the conflict between the theory of free will and the law of conservation of energy.

The sub could not believe it. The pack of cards strewn over the table, and only half hidden by the hastily-arranged cloth, the pile of cigarette stubs in the fireplace, and the all-night face of the man opposite, were all contradictions. It almost seemed as if these men were trying to make him think that they cared for nothing but study and church.

Now Corydon cared no more and no less than the average youth for an excess of either of these two very necessary things, and this soon became tiresome. So he rose, and said he thought that he would have to go.

"Oh, don't be in a hurry," said Puggy, in dismay. "You 've just come."

"I must, thank you. I have an examination to-morrow, you know," said Corydon, moving toward the door.

"That 's so — well, can't I show you your way to the car?"

"Oh, no! — thank you; but I — I know the way all right," protested the sub, with trepidation as he thought of the waiting rarebit.

"We 're awfully glad to have seen you," said Hollister.

"Can't you dine with us to-morrow?" asked the crew man.

"I promised to call on Mr. Hildreth after the examination," hesitated Corydon.

"Go there first. We don't lunch until one, and you 'll be through on the hill by eleven."

"Come on," added the *Cornellian* editor, and he weakly gave in.

As their guest vanished into the night, and, unseen, into the Rho Tau camp, Puggy Workman walked slowly back to the reception-room.

He leaned against the mantel, and looked at Hollister. "Jake," said he, finally, "something is wrong. Have we lost our cunning? That man was bored."

"I should have played those hymns," said Wilbur, shuffling the cards.

"And then you'd been bored," said Hollister, grimly. "Good-night."

. . . .

It was after twelve when Melville E. Corydon, tired, but happy, tumbled into bed at the Ithaca Hotel. The day had been full of many momentous happenings for him, and he had met so many men that their faces danced before his eyes like the pictures on a kinetoscope. He had seen two fraternities, and liked the men in both. To-morrow he was to see them both again, and another besides. What would be the outcome? Would he receive an invitation from any of them? And if more than one asked him, which, if any, should he accept? So far he liked the Rho Taus the better. They seemed more attached to each other and more congenial to him. Then, too, there was the football team and the Banjo Club, and, possibly, the baseball team. It might be well, if he were going to try for any of them — and Torresdale and Blake both wanted him to try — to get the advantage of any points they might give him.

He liked the Beta Chis, too, but he hoped they would treat him differently the next time he saw them. There *was* such a thing as too much study and church, he thought. He would wait. He would see what they really were like. He would not be in a hurry. That was what Pritchard had told him — not to be in a hurry. He remembered that he had crooked his forefinger at him to emphasize his words. What a funny nose Pritchard had! And then he went to sleep.

At eight o'clock on the following morning Thorpe, ever-watchful, peered in through the library lecture-room window, and saw him busily frowning over his examination. Thorpe had chanced to meet him on the campus, and had introduced him to Cooley, who was also an entering freshman, and, as he proudly explained to Corydon, who found him a very congenial companion and bound by a bond of sympathy, pledged Rho Tau. Corydon noticed the enamelled button fastened in the lapel of his coat, and was told that it was a pledge button. He was told, also, many other things he had not known, and, coming from a sub like himself, he did not question their truth. He learned more of the fraternities and of the system of rushing, and he learned that the only society really worth joining was Rho Tau. Beta Chi and Chi Delta Sigma were good, Cooley said, but not to be compared with Rho Tau; and Cooley said this, not because he was pledged Rho Tau, but because it was his honest conviction, and he really believed it. Moreover, it was generally conceded. All Rho Tau men, either in this chapter or in any other, were gentlemen, and you were sure to like them. Also at all the colleges, which Rho Tau had seen fit to honor with a chapter, that chapter was easily the first and most prominent of any there. The alumni of Rho Tau were more loyal than the alumni of any other society. The bond between Rho Taus was stronger than the bond of any of the rest.

Of course Corydon could not know that Thorpe had routed the pledged man out of bed at six o'clock that morning, and had impressed him with many instructions; and, of course, he could not know that the meeting on the campus had been deliberately planned. Therefore the stock of Rho Tau slid up fifty points.

When at last he handed in his paper with a sigh, he smiled with the smile known only to the man who has "hit it." He had answered every question, and his heart was light. He walked down the hill, wondering joyously over what Cooley had told him of fraternities; and when Hildreth hailed him from the piazza of the Chi Delt house he started guiltily, for, in his ecstasy, he had forgotten his engagement.

"Hallo, there, Corydon," said Hildreth, as

the sub came up the steps. "Were n't going to shake us, were you?"

Corydon explained.

"That so?" said Hildreth, heartily. "Well! Glad you hit it. That English exam. is sometimes a corker. Come around and sit down and smoke a cigarroon. Jack Fordyce is here."

They walked around the corner of the piazza, where Fordyce and six or eight other youths were reclining with railinged feet and studying the summer sky. Fordyce rose as he saw the sub.

"Hello, old man," said he, "glad to see you. Just getting down the hill?"

Corydon admitted it, and, as the rest uncoiled themselves, Hildreth performed the necessary introductions and waved him to a chair. The sub sat down and waited. Fordyce gave him a cigarette and bade him smoke; and for a while he puffed in silence and listened.

The Chi Delts believed that the best way in which to make a man feel at home was to treat him with no special consideration, and with the same degree of courtesy they showed each other. In this way they claimed to eradicate the "being rushed" feeling from the mind of the man they were entertaining, and to make him act naturally. The man usually felt rather uncomfortable; but this they claimed was also natural. They shared in the general belief, however, that the freshman, to be conquered, must be met on his own ground, and it was for this reason that Corydon, whom they believed, on good information, to be of somewhat speedy tendencies, was regaled that morning with stories of a more or less questionable character, and tales of swift experiences, shared in by most of the men.

As usual, he found himself next to the fraternity celebrity. This time he was a long individual, who masqueraded under the euphonious title of "Bug." Corydon, noticing his blue serge coat, with the crossed oars embroidered in white silk above the pocket, asked if he was connected with the 'varsity crew, and learned that his honor was that of conversing with the Commodore of the Cornell Navy.

After that he learned that there were two Banjo and one Mandolin Club man among them, and that Hildreth was the first baseman on the team. The array was somewhat imposing.

But what puzzled the sub-freshman most was the insistency with which they all told stories of their own bold and dark deeds, and how they disputed when Hildreth claimed to have, on a certain evidently memorable night, drunk three more glasses of whiskey than the Mandolin Club man. He began to think that this crowd was rather speedy. He, at school, had always been the last to condemn anything of that sort; but he felt that there was a limit,—just as there was a limit to which one might comfortably go in the other direction. He was thinking of the Beta Chis just then.

Yet he did not refuse the crackers and wine which, at a sign from Fordyce, the trig little negro boy placed on the wicker table. He had no way of knowing that this was the only bottle in the house, and had been bought for the occasion. And he did not refuse the cordial invitation that the crew man gave him as he was leaving.

All this was because the sub was continuing to learn. He recognized the value of a society, since his talk with Cooley, and he realized fully that he was being rushed. Therefore he believed he could best serve his own interests by making up his mind as soon as possible, that there might be no hesitancy if he should be asked. To this end he must not refuse invitations from any of them, and, once accepted, they must not be broken.

So Corydon went up to the Beta Chi house to lunch, and after he had lunched he went to his hotel; and when he reached his hotel he found an invitation to the Rho Tau house to dinner, and he went up the long hill again.

Thus things went on. One day he would go sailing with the Rho Taus, driving with the Chi Delts, and swimming with the Beta Chis. All the other societies kept their hands off and watched. The next day he would go calling with the Rho Taus, playing tennis with the Chi

Delts, and dining with the Beta Chis. The rushing grew hot and fierce, and the sub was foxy, and showed no preference. The Rho Taus, to make a ten strike, gave a dance for him. The Chi Delts, not to be outdone, gave a huge dinner, with many bottles thereat, at Kay's. The Beta Chis, to cap the climax, invited the Episcopal minister, his wife, and the superintendent of the Sunday-school to dinner to meet him. Corydon went to them all, one after another.

The sub was a lion.

Finally the Beta Chis cornered him one afternoon, and with much *empressement* and solemnity offered him an election. They expatiated on their position in college; they pointed to their long and growing chapter-roll with pride; they bore down upon their intimacy with certain professors, whom Corydon had met at their house, and they trotted the crew man, the *Cornellian* editor, and a bunch of lesser satellites back and forth until Corydon's vision blurred and dimmed. They dwelt on their own steadiness, and they asked Corydon to say frankly whether he believed any other crowd better, morally, than they. When Corydon said that, so far as he had seen, they were better than the rest, that way, they looked at each other in triumph, and Hollister sighed as he thought how soon the strain would be over.

But when Corydon said that he could not make up his mind yet, that he must have time, they looked startled and grieved. They did not understand, they said, why he hesitated; and for a while they seriously considered taking back their invitation. Later, when they found him immovable against all bluffs, they graciously permitted him ten days in which to decide.

So Corydon waited. A day after his interview with the Beta Chis, Hildreth and Fordyce called on him at the hotel, and, with many throat-clearings and looks of mystery, explained their mission, — that of offering him the honor of an election to Chi Delta Sigma. They showed him wherein they were superior to all others. They assured him that in no other crowd would he find such close relationship among the members. They asked him if he did not consider their crowd far livelier than the others; and when he told them that, as far as he knew, they certainly were, Fordyce looked at Hildreth, and Hildreth looked at Fordyce, both with smiles of satisfaction.

When Corydon thanked them for the honor, but told them that he could not yet decide, they gasped.

"Can't decide! Why — why! I — " said Fordyce.

"Corydon, think carefully," said Hildreth. "People don't get invitations to Chi Delta Sigma every day."

"I *have* thought, Mr. Hildreth," answered the sub. "I simply can't arrive at any conclusion at present. I like your men very much indeed, and I appreciate the honor of your invitation. But what can I do? I don't know what I want myself, yet."

"You only think you don't, old man," said Fordyce, pulling himself together, and putting his hand on Corydon's knee. "You really want Chi Delta Sigma — as badly as we want you. Listen!" and Fordyce began to talk.

He talked in a low, impressive tone, at first, and, as he went on, it grew vibrant and pleading. Corydon was sorry; sorry because he liked Fordyce very much and hated to disappoint him by his answer, and sorry because Fordyce's earnestness and feeling made it doubly hard for him to keep the resolution he had made. Twice he was on the verge of yielding, and twice, in the very knick of time, despite Fordyce's impassioned tones, the faces of Torresdale and Thorpe rose before him, and he drew back on the very brink. It was not strange that his resolutions should be so nearly broken, for Fordyce was one of the best talkers and most able elocutionists in college, and many a sub, just as full of resolve as Corydon, had gone down before his all-powerful tongue. But Corydon straightened up and shook himself.

"Mr. Fordyce," said he, "you 're making this

hard for me. Please don't. I've got to have time."

So Fordyce stopped. Hildreth suggested that a drink might be in order; but Corydon, who wanted to be alone, and think, excused himself; and the two Chi Delts, with an expressed hope and an unexpressed fear, left him.

"Jack," said Hildreth, as they left the hotel, "that lad is no one's fool, if he *is* a sport."

"Right," said Fordyce. "That's our play, though. He seems to pay more attention to our apparent gayness than to anything else. We'll keep it up."

Meanwhile Corydon stood looking out of the window, and wrinkling his subbish young forehead in thought.

In the last few days he had made inquiries here and there, and had learned of the standing of the three fraternities, relatively to the rest of the college. Of the three he infinitely preferred Rho Tau; but as Rho Tau had not yet honored him with an invitation, and as he did not know that he would be so favored, he was in something of a quandary. He realized that his stay in Ithaca was of short duration, and that he could not hold his two present invitations over the summer. If Rho Tau asked him before he left, he would pledge himself. If they did not, he must decide whether he would accept one of the others, or let them both go, in the hope of being asked in the fall by Rho Tau. What was best?

In his perplexity he thought of Torresdale. He had been asked to dinner by Thorpe that evening, and he would doubtless see the football man there. Torresdale had once, in a long, serious talk about fraternities, and things concerning which Corydon wished to learn, told him not to hesitate if there ever was anything he wished to know, but to come to him and let him help him out with his greater experience. Here was a chance to test his good faith. He would go to Torresdale, not as a freshman to a senior, but as a man to a man, and he would ask him what he thought was best to do.

It was remarkably lucky for Melville E.

Corydon that his resolution was forestalled. Seniors do not court man to man conversations about their fraternities with sub-freshmen, and Mr. Corydon would most surely have seen his chances for Rho Tau vanish in the dimmest part of the dim distance, had he held his proposed court of inquiry.

As it was, when he sought out Torresdale after dinner, and asked for the privilege of a few minutes' conversation with him, Torresdale said pleasantly, —

"Why, of course. I have something to say to you, too, which might as well be said now as at any time. Let's go up in my study," and, as he led the way, he shot a glance at the group around the piano, which meant "no interruptions, please."

Corydon sat down and cleared his throat. He did not know just where to begin. Somehow it was harder to say than he had thought, when he had considered the matter at his hotel. He watched Torresdale lighting his pipe, and he cleared his throat again.

Then Torresdale spoke. "Perhaps," said he, "you had better let me say my little piece first. Afterwards, I'll be willing to help you in any way I can."

The sub was only too glad of the brief respite, and he prepared to listen. Torresdale commenced.

He did not have the ready flow of words in which Fordyce rejoiced, and he did not use the awe-inspiring solemnity of Hollister; but as Corydon heard what the big guard was saying, with his simple straightforward earnestness, his heart began to swell, and his vision became blurred. Torresdale started at the beginning. He told the sub something of the society and its policy. He told of its foundation years ago. He spoke of some of the alumni who had gone from the sheltering walls of the chapter-house to rise among their fellowmen in the world outside. He said something of each of the different men in the house, and he spoke of them as one brother would of another. Then as Corydon, scarcely breathing, lest he lose a word, bent forward in his chair, he began to tell him that they wanted him to be among them next year and forever after. He said that he had been commissioned by every man in the society to extend the offer of membership to him, and his voice sank deep into Corydon's soul as he ended with "and it is the warmest wish of all of us that you accept. We want you, and we hope that you want us, and, from my own experience, I do not hesitate to say that if you pledge yourself you will never, on this earth, or on any other, regret your decision."

Corydon looked up and met Torresdale's eyes. Then he looked around the room for a moment. Then he looked up again, and, with a sudden impulsive movement, held out his hand. Torresdale grasped it tightly. "Will you?" he asked quickly.

Melville R. Corydon, sub-freshman, put his hand on the senior's shoulder. This was very fresh.

"Will I?" he said, with a queer little laugh. "Torry, I was afraid you would not ask me."

Torresdale gave an exultant chuckle, and, flinging wide the door, filled the house with a series of exultant roars.

Doors opened, and men swarmed from everywhere. They rattled down from the third story and up from the first, and, as they came, they whooped. Torresdale stood by the door and laughed more softly as the men came pouring into the room. Corydon did not quite understand; but he was glad to have all the fellows shaking his hand and telling him how glad they were.

.   .   .   .

On the following day, as Puggy Workman was basking in the sun, on the Beta Chi house piazza, there came a freshman to him with his mail.

In it were the following letters.

FORTUNATUS CONSTANTINE WORKMAN,
 BETA CHI HOUSE, ITHACA, N. Y.

MY DEAR SON, — I have received no acknowledgment of the draft I sent you over a week

5   65

ago. Please let me know at once whether you received it.

Aff't'ly,

FATHER.

P. S. I made a slight misstatement in my last letter to you. I told you, if I remember rightly, that R. E. Corydon's son was going to Ithaca to take his entrance examinations. This, I found later, was a mistake on my part. The young man who is there is, as you doubtless know by this time, the son of Mr. R. F. Corydon, and is not the ardent church-worker I supposed. In fact, I do not believe he is overly attentive to his spiritual welfare.   F.

F. C. WORKMAN, ESQ.,
   BETA CHI HOUSE, CITY.

DEAR MR. WORKMAN, — It is with many thanks to you, and a great deal of regret on my part, that I tell you that I must decline the honor conferred upon me by your society in asking me to join. It has been a hard matter for me to decide between three fraternities, and in pledging myself Rho Tau I have followed my inclinations as nearly as I knew how.

I trust that the cordial relations established between us will not entirely cease because I have chosen as I have, and I thank you all most heartily for your hospitality.

> Very truly,
>
> MELVILLE R. CORYDON.

Later in the day the snub-nosed boy brought another message to Hildreth. It read: —

WM. A. HILDRETH,
  CHI DELTA SIGMA HOUSE, ITHACA, N. Y.

Corydon, son of R. F., not R. A. Not sporty. Good fellow and fine football player. Rush hard. Sorry. My mistake.

> PIKE.

This came collect. Ten minutes later another mail came, and with it another letter.

W. A. HILDRETH, ESQ.,
  CHI DELTA SIGMA HOUSE, CITY.

DEAR MR. HILDRETH, — It is with many thanks to you, and a great deal of regret on my part, that I tell you that I must decline the honor conferred upon me by your society in asking me to join. It has been a hard matter for me to decide between two fraternities, and in pledging myself Rho Tau I have followed my inclinations as nearly as I knew how.

I trust that the cordial relations established between us will not entirely cease because I have chosen as I have, and I thank you all most heartily for your hospitality.

Very truly,

MELVILLE R. CORYDON.

That night Beta Chi and Chi Delta Sigma broke training.

LITTLE TYLER

LITTLE TYLER

THEY were waiting in front of the drug-store for a car. Torresdale was going to football practice, and Little Tyler, trotting dog-like at his heels, was going to look on.

Little Tyler was very proud that day, for it was something to know the crack-guard of the 'varsity; and it was more to know him well, to be seen with him, and to be permitted to carry his moleskins. He ran along by his side, look-ing up into his face, and drinking, open-mouthed, every word, as he talked of the different players in an easy, familiar way. He even called the captain of the 'varsity by his first name; and to Little Tyler there was no one quite so awful as the captain of the 'varsity. He stood on a pedestal among his men, and looked down on the college with a far-off, affable condescension that did not seem at all like an ordinary man. Little Tyler had watched him. Often, as the captain stood in front of Lincoln Hall, between recitations, talking to other seniors in that deep, heavy voice of his, he had edged as close to the group as he dared, and caught fragments of mysterious conversations about a certain Bobby and his problems; and sometimes in the long nights, when he had been unable to sleep because of the pain in his back, he had lain in bed practising his intonations and tones, feeling all the time as if he were committing a sacrilege. Once, when he had been walking up the campus with Torresdale, the captain had passed them, and said, "'Lo, Torry," and "How are you, Tyler?" as he brushed by. This was the nearest he had ever come to knowing him; but he had shivered all over with joy, and had lived on that memory for weeks.

In the same way, though with a slightly less degree of reverence, he admired Torresdale. Torresdale was a freshman, and in his own class, so that of course he was not now nearly

so far above him as the captain. He felt
certain that even if the skies should fall, or the
whole earth should change in some way, so
that he should know the captain very well, he
should never be able to talk to him and ask
him things as he could Torresdale. Not that
Torresdale was at all an ordinary person, but
because he was a freshman, — and all freshmen
are kin, — and possibly because he had been
very kind to him, and had tried never to do
anything that would remind him of that ugly
hump on his back.

For weeks, his admiration had fallen from
afar, and had confined itself to wistfully watching Torresdale's figure, as he swung up the
campus or ran around the track with the training
squad. There was a hope in his heart that he
might some day know him; and at first, when
Torresdale was only playing on the scrub, this
had not seemed impossible; but later, when he
had been chosen for the 'varsity, his heart sank
and hope died, for he had never dreamed of
knowing a real 'varsity football player.

Being freshmen, they both happened to be in the same five-hour math. section, and one day Torresdale came late to the recitation in trigonometry. Partly through accident, and partly because he had noticed the bent little figure with the pinched-looking face and wistful eyes, he had dropped into the seat next him, and had nodded pleasantly. Little Tyler, his heart beating a stifling tattoo against his ribs, nodded back, scarcely knowing what he did; and little by little they had fallen into a whispered conversation, roughly broken by the instructor's sudden turning and asking for order in an extremely unpleasant tone. Then he shrank back in his seat and looked frightened. Torresdale had only smiled and remarked, in a husky and very audible whisper, that "Old Stone" had his back up this morning. He had learned what instructors were for, and "Old Stone" evidently knew it, for he did not turn again. By the end of the hour they were on the best of terms; and after that Torresdale had always smiled and nodded, and often sat beside him. One day

they had met on the campus, and Torresdale
had suggested that Little Tyler should take
dinner with him that evening. Little Tyler
had gone, and they had sat talking football
until far into the night. Day by day the
friendship grew. Torresdale, with his big,
overflowing heart, learned to await the coming
of the little hunchback, and learned what it
really was to watch over and be thoughtful for
some one else. It was rather a new sensation,
and he liked it. He liked to talk and watch
the little thin face light up, and the wistful,
deep-set eyes glow and sparkle when he told of
some exciting tackle or wonderful run; and he
found out, too, that there were few men on the
team who knew more about the theories of football than Little Tyler.

On the other hand, Little Tyler, who had
never in all his life known what it was to have
a real chum, looked up to Torresdale as to a
god, and worshipped him with a blind devo-
tion. The rest of the men in his class, and the
others whom he had known before he came to

college, had always treated him as a child.
Torresdale gave his years due credit and respect;
but the rest, partly on account of an uncon-
fessed feeling of embarrassment in the presence
of his misfortune, and partly because they had
never tried to know him, refused him admittance
to their fellowship. They never noticed him
when they were planning cider raids or flag
raisings, for he could be of no use to them in
such things. They never noticed him in class
meetings, for he could not stand boldly forth,
as did the rest, and make enthusiastic, burning
speeches about the tyrannical sophomores, and
what the class would do if given the chance.
He was usually wedged in between two men,
and almost out of sight, so that no one ever
knew how his cheeks burned and his fingers
itched to be well and strong, that he might
do his share and show his class spirit. They
did not need him; and in their life his pitiful,
misshapen figure acted as a wet blanket on all
their fun.

But Torresdale treated him as an equal. He

did not patronize him when he spoke, but asked his advice on lots of things, and talked to him just as though he were one of the others who could stand up straight. His whole heart went out to him. It was good to have some one talk to him as though he were a man, and like to have him around; it was better that the some one was the right-guard of the football team; it was best of all that he was Torresdale. Had he been given his choice of all his class, he would have chosen no one else. Torresdale was so clever, so big, so warm-hearted. There was no one so popular or so handsome among all the freshmen. No one else dared to talk to the professors in that easy way he had. Decidedly, there was no one among all the under-classmen who was quite so great and good as Torresdale.

Through the occult method of communication known by freshmen and sophomores, the news had swept through class-room and campus that on this night there would be a fierce rush on Eddy Street. In consequence, the feeling between the two classes had raged all day long at fever heat. No one knew who were the leaders in the movement, but every one felt the need of an old-time rush to clear the air. The valiant sophomores, stern in the sense of their class duty, and bold in the remembrance of their preceding year's victory, had been too long overbearing, and the under-class, at first timid with the sense of new surroundings and unfamiliar traditions, had found itself. Under the guidance and advice of friendly juniors the class had organized, for there had been too much of the humiliating drinking of milk and vinegar forced down one's throat by a big sophomore and a rubber tube, and it was time they earned their rightful emancipation.

There had been a number of other rushes in the earlier part of the term, but they had been battles between veterans, and half the number of raw troops, and the sophomores had easily won. This time, things were to be different. The flag was to be of the stoutest painted canvas, strong enough to bear an enormous strain. The strongest men in the freshman class, including Torresdale, were to lay tight hold of the flag on one side, while the three chosen from the sophomores seized the other. Then a senior gave the word, and both classes were to rush together and fight for its possession. It promised to be very interesting, and the jaded seniors and juniors, behind whom active participancy in such affairs lay, looked forward to a very pleasant evening.

Torresdale and Little Tyler were talking about it. The latter held the big guard's moleskin football trousers hugged affectionately to his breast, and looked up awfully into his face as he spoke of the horrors, the delights, and the probable perils of the coming evening.

"And it will be the biggest rush ever," he finally ended, standing with his legs apart, and tapping Little Tyler solemnly on the shoulder, — "absolutely the biggest rush ever. There will be blood, and lots of it. The bodies will sway, and sophomores will be trampled upon and groan horribly. Ah-h-h-h!" and

Torresdale clicked his teeth together in anticipation.

"Shall we really win?" asked Little Tyler, anxiously, — "shall we *really?*"

"If I thought we should n't," replied Torresdale, slowly, "I would never show my face at Percy Field again. I would never touch a football again. Never — though they offered to make me captain three times over — if I thought we should n't. But I don't."

"That's *good*," said Little Tyler. "And you are in the middle, Torry? Who were chosen with you?"

"Johnson on my right and H. Lockwood on my left. They are two of the huskiest men in college," answered Torresdale. "There are only three men in the whole sophomore class of whom we need be at all afraid."

"Birdsell, Humboldt, and who else?" asked Little Tyler, timidly.

"Why, how in the deuce did you know who I meant?" said Torresdale, staring. "Dickson is the other. But how did you know?"

"I've watched them playing on the scrub when I've been down," apologized Little Tyler. "The first two are hard men, I imagine; but Dickson missed three tackles last week Friday, and his shoulders are too narrow. He won't last, I think."

"H'm," said his companion, looking down at him curiously. "Perhaps you're right. Still, that six-handed business is not the main issue. As soon as the word is given, we shall, of course, try to get that flag, but we won't be the only ones. In less than ten seconds, there will be a close, howling mob around us, and every one will be fighting for a grip on it. One side will pull one way, and one the other, and it won't be any easy job for any one."

"Oh, I *wish* I were strong! I *wish* I could be in that!" cried Little Tyler, quickly. He clasped his hands, and looked beseechingly up at his friend, who towered above him like a giant over a pigmy. "Torry, you're the only one that knows. The others think I have no class spirit, because I can't talk and go into athletics, and do the other things they do. They think I am a coward because of that," he jerked his head backwards toward his bent, deformed back, — "a coward," he whispered. "Do you hear, Torry? — a *coward!*"

Torresdale dropped his hand on his shoulder. "Hush, Tyler," he said. "I know it's hard, and d—d hard, too. It must be. But you stick it out. There is not one man in twenty who would have dared to try college at all, if he — if he — were like you. I'm not blind; and maybe I've seen more than you think. They don't mean it. They simply don't understand. Wait! They will in time; and if you can show the courage to force them to understand, you will be happy all your life. If you leave college, no one will ever know you were not what some of them may be short-sighted enough to think you now. You *stay*, and — and — well, *I'm* here, you know."

"I know, Torry," said the hunchback, gratefully; "I'm sorry I spoke as I did. It was weak, and I don't think I'll do it again. At

least, I 'll try not. Just forget, will you, please?
But I 'm going to show them, I 'll show them,
if it kills me."

Torresdale eyed him keenly. " You keep out
of that rush," he said. " Mind! "

Little Tyler laughed.

At the field that day he sat in state on the
side lines, with Torresdale's coat over his knees,
and his 'varsity sweater, red with the big white
C in the centre, tied snugly around his neck by
the sleeves. No one paid any attention to him,
and he sat alone, eagerly watching the plays,
and applauding with his shrill little voice and
thin hands whenever his beloved Torry smashed
huge holes in the line and the backs darted
through for gains. Day after day, the humped-
up little figure had followed the team's every
movement, and he knew the strong and weak
points as well as though he had been the head-
coach himself. He knew that Lyndhurst, the
right end, played out too far, and he doubled
his fists in agony every time a back shot through
the line, between him and the tackle. He saw

that the right half-back was too slow in starting, and that the left ran too high, and hit the
line sideways. He found out, by the way in
which the scrub full-back placed himself, just
before the plays when the 'varsity had the ball,
that he knew all the 'varsity signals, and he
wanted to tell the captain, but did not dare.
He was afraid it would be fresh and interfer-
ing, and he thought that the captain, who had
forgotten more about football than he had ever
dreamed of knowing, must know it anyway.
It was so plain, he thought, that not noticing
was impossible; so he sat still and said nothing.

Between the halves the coaches took the men
off in one corner of the field, and talked to them
earnestly. They gathered in a circle, with their
heads together and their hands on each other's
shoulders, while the head-coach stood in the
centre and talked. Little Tyler could see his
arms waving up and down, and he grinned out
of the sleeves of his sweater, for he knew the
coach had seen what he had seen, and was trying, in his own vigorous way, to correct it.

It was the first day of November, and the chilly autumn winds swept over the field. Up on Dead Head Hill the trees, from which the townies and little muckers were wont to see the games, waved their huge arm-like branches against the gray eastern sky, like the tentacles of an enormous octopus. The leaves blew in little whirlwinds all along the fence, and the windows of the clubhouse rattled and chattered with every gust, as if protesting against the rudeness of the wind. Sweatered and overcoated students stood with their hands in their pockets, shiveringly waiting for play to begin again; and over near the main entrance Jack, the keeper of the field, seated on his big iron roller, was swearing gloriously at his cherished horse, than which, as he explained, on every possible occasion, there was not a — finer — horse in the whole — town of Ithaca, by — !

Little Tyler grew cold and lonely as he waited. He tied the sweater more tightly, and burrowed down into his overcoat. He wished some one of those freshmen who were kicking

that borrowed football around over there by the
goalposts would come over and speak to him,
and treat him as though he really belonged to
the class and was somebody. He would prove
to them, if they would only give him the
chance, that he was just as loyal and as eager
as they that the class should be great; but they
did not seem to care what he thought. He
would have died before he would have walked
up to them and joined them, as two or three
other freshmen had done, and as all freshmen
should do, because he realized his infirmity, and
was keenly sensitive to their observation; but
he *did* wish that one or two of them would come
voluntarily to him, just because they wanted to
see him and talk to him. He had been in college now for almost two whole months, and
during all that time had met, outside of Torresdale, only ten of his class. Every one knew
who *he* was because he happened to be a curiosity in college; but his natural reserve, coupled
with his diffidence and pride, had made them
think that he did not wish companionship, and

they avoided him. Those few who had talked with him liked him and went out of their way to send a morning "Hello" at him as they met in their classes; but the others, simply because he looked so queer, believed that he must be different and unlike them in tastes and inclinations, so they had taken the surest course to shut him out from their hearts and fellowship, — that of not making his acquaintance.

There was no way for them to know that Little Tyler was sitting with Torresdale's coat over his knees, internally crying his heart out (and biting his upper lip hard to keep from doing it externally), because he was not as they were, and because it had been decreed that he never should be. They did not know how many nights he had tossed in his bed and clenched his hands to prevent himself from getting up and writing home to say he could not stand it, and was coming back. Torresdale would never tell, because he never knew. Little Tyler would never show it, because he was too proud. The class would never find it out, because men, never looking, seldom know what their fellows are suffering.

Most men who had passed through such an experience would have been bitter against their class and its members. The constant ignorance of his existence as a man and a freshman would have driven most men back into themselves, but with Little Tyler it was different. He was used to reticence, and accustomed to being ignored. As far back as his memory reached, he had been of no account. He could not remember when his little misshapen figure had ever produced any other results in the world, and he was wise enough to know that his physical appearance had made him unconsciously sensitive and proud. He knew also that these were two reasons within himself that forbade his breathing just the same air that his classmates did.

But as he sat there after the second half, waiting for Torresdale to dress and join him, his thoughts ran riot through his brain. He tried to puzzle it all out. Why were things so?

Why was there not some way to show them
that he was as much flesh and blood as they?
And if there was not, why were people made
with backs that did not fit? He had been very
brave, up there with Torresdale, when he had
said that he would show them; but it was one
thing to talk and another to act. He could n't
just go up and chum with them, as the others
did, so there was an end to that. He could n't
stand up and talk in class meeting. He was
sure of that. If he stood on the floor he looked
more bent than ever; if he stood on a bench he
looked ridiculous. What was there for him to
do? Was it always to be this way? Could
he never get into their hearts? How could
he break the ice and win a little, just a very
little, of their fellowship? If he could help
the class in any way, it would be above everything best, and he should like that; but how
was *he* to help the class? There was the rush.
Torresdale had told him to keep out of that.
Torry must think he was a fool! What a lot
of use he would be in a rush! He would only

be in every one's way — that was it, — in every
one's way. He had always been in every one's
way!

He wondered if Torry thought that; and, at
the idea, a great lump rose in his throat as he
looked forlornly across the windy field. No,
there was no use. He would always remain
the little bent and useless hunchback. No one
would ever think that he amounted to anything. No one besides Torry would ever want
him around. It was hard, — it was very hard, and
yet he was afraid that it was awfully, terribly
true. Of what use was he? He couldn't even
study so as to get a prize; and, anyway, what
good would that do? He might just as well
make up his mind now, either to stay and stick
it out and be miserably unhappy, or to go home
defeated, which would not be pleasant. Neither
way would be pleasant, but — Oh, *would* all
his life be this way? Would he be always just
outside and never just in? He was afraid to
look forward to the next three years. If a
change of some sort did not soon take place, he

should do something he ought not. He felt it. He did not know what it would be, but he should do it. At least, people would notice him then— Oh, what *was* he talking about, and where was Torresdale? He had been sitting on that damp ground long enough, and he should be here by this time. If he did not come, he should go on home and not wait.

Torresdale came across the field, whistling gayly. His cheeks were red, and his long, curly football hair blew in the wind. Little Tyler handed him his sweater in silence, and he pulled it over his head. From its depths his big cheerful voice plumped out, "Well— what do you think?"

Little Tyler got up. His legs were stiff from the cold ground. "I don't think I can, Torry," he said slowly.

Torresdale stared, and then laughed. It was a round, whole-souled, healthy laugh. "Don't you, indeed?" he said. "*I* was talking about football."

"Oh," said little Tyler, wearily, "Lyndhurst

plays too far out, and the backs are slow. Let's go home."

"Humph," grunted his friend, "what's the matter with you?"

"Nothing," answered Little Tyler, "only — let's go home."

Torresdale picked up his football suit. It was his intention to be armored in the rush, and the oddly-assorted pair started off together.

Going through the archway they passed Jack, on his roller, and the big guard shouted a good-natured inquiry as to the state of health of his horse. Jack rumbled back, seriously advising Torresdale, as a physician, to go — south for the winter, and Torresdale chuckled joyously. Back of the gun factory they left the road; and, picking their way among the straw stacks, mounted the long flight of steps leading to the top of the bluff. Neither spoke, but once or twice Little Tyler caught his breath with a little quick gasp, for the climb was hard for him. Torresdale heard it, and, with a sudden pang, called himself a brute for forgetting and not riding home. When they reached the spring at the summit, he pretended to be most thirsty, and spent several minutes in hunting for the dipper, while Little Tyler sat on a rock and rested. Then they started on again, cross lots, over the fields, and down back of the University buildings.

That evening Torresdale stood alone in his room, lacing on his canvas jacket. His mind and heart were full of the coming rush, for, next to his fraternity, he loved his class far better than anything else in college, and to-night he was to help defend its honor. But a few minutes before, Billy Smith, the president of the junior class, had stopped him as he came down from dinner, and told him that the whole class was looking at him, and that he must not fail. There was no need to tell *him* that, he said to himself, as he savagely pulled at the lacings. He would — tug — hang on, tug — to that — tug — flag until he died. He guessed he knew what an important part he played in this show; and if he did not do his share, it would be very queer indeed. He dipped his hands again in the powdered resin on the table, and gave himself a little shake, just to feel his strength, and sat down by the window to wait for Billy Smith and the other two men. Billy Smith was to look them all over, and give them a few pointers just before they all went to the battlefield; and he had told Torresdale on no account to leave before he came. So he sat still and waited.

Outside, the supressed excitement and feeling that had filled the air all day began to find vent in occasional class yells and howls of derision, as a group of sophomores passed a knot of freshmen. In the darkness Torresdale could see the figures of men pouring from the different boarding houses out into Heustis Street. Some went straight down Dryden Road to Eddy. Others stood in bunches of ten or fifteen, yelling, "Ninety Blank, this way!" or "Ninety Dash, *this* way!" A few isolated men wandered around, trying to place themselves with their own class. It was fun, Torresdale thought, to see them edge quietly up to a group, and duck and dart away at the sight of an unfamiliar face, or the utterance of an antagonistic sentiment. Occasionally, once or twice, two groups, unable to restrain themselves longer, charged together and developed miniature rushes; but these were always quickly nipped in the bud by the upper-classmen, who patrolled the streets, secure in the dignity of their extra years. "Hold on!" they would command grandly; "you'll have all the fighting you want later!" The upper-classmen were not going to have their fun spoiled.

Once the door of a boarding-house was opened for a moment, and in the flood of lamplight that fell across the sidewalk Torresdale saw Humboldt, his chief opponent, talking to five other sophomores. Torresdale shut his teeth hard. He did not like Humboldt, and Humboldt knew it. There would be a big fight there, he said to himself. He had just time to notice that he wore a leather belt around his waist before the door closed. A moment afterwards· two of the freshman groups caught sight of him at the window, and yelled to him. He shouted back, and the next second heard them give his class cheer with his name at the end. It made him feel cold and shivery, and it made him shut his hands over an imaginary flag, and say, beneath his breath, "They sha'n't — they sha'n't!" Then the two groups moved on and left him. In the lull that followed, he had just time to wonder where Billy Smith was, with H. Lockwood and Johnson, and to wish that they would hurry.

Suddenly from the darkness below there came a faint little cry.

"Torry! — oh, Torry!"

Torresdale shut his teeth with a snap. In the excitement he had forgotten all about Little Tyler, and for the first time, since he had known him, he felt that he did not want him around. He did not want any but able-bodied men that night, he said once more to himself. Why could he not have had more sense? He ought to have known that he would be in the way. So Torresdale drew his head in and kept very quiet.

In a moment the voice rose again, and this time it was thrilled and shrill with excitement, and there was an appeal in it that Torresdale could not forego. He swore to himself, and stuck his head out ungraciously.

"Hello, Tyler. What do you want?" he said.

"Oh, Torry, I did not mean to bother you to-night — really, I did n't; but Billy Smith says for you to come down at once. He has Johnson and H. Lockwood with him!" cried the voice.

"Oh!" said Torresdale, with a sudden change that did not escape notice below, "wait a minute."

A second later the lights went out, and two seconds after that Torresdale stood on the side-walk. "Come on," he said briefly, and started away at a tremendous pace down the hill to Eddy Street. Little Tyler ran by his side in little halting jumps. As they turned the corner, the rising moon was just showing itself over

7

the western hills. It made a silver road across
the black lake far below, and its light streamed
down over the housetops. In the centre of its
strength there stood a mighty crowd of sophomores and freshmen, surging and swaying to
and fro, and exchanging taunts and jeers.
The freshmen were huddled together in one
solid crowd; but the sophomores, more used to
the situation, were spread out, and laughed and
talked together to show their confidence. A
space of about thirty feet divided them; and
seniors and juniors, watching warily for any
outbreak, held them back, waiting for the
proper time. The faces of the nearest shone
white and tense in the moonlight; and, as the
whole scene spread itself before the two men
coming down the hill, they paused.

"That's *good*," said Little Tyler.

"Hurry up, Torresdale! We 're waiting for
you," some junior cried; and Torresdale, forgetting all else, broke into a run, letting Little
Tyler follow as best he might.

"This way, Torresdale," yelled Billy Smith;

and Torresdale went over to receive Billy's explanations and his own last instructions with his co-gladiators.

"Sorry," said Smith, "I was detained. Did Little Tyler get you all right?"

"Uh-huh!" grunted Torresdale. "Did you say to take hold this way?"

"Put your hands a little more apart. So! That's it. Now just keep your wits about you, and you will be all right."

"Where are the others?" asked the guard, practising his new-taught hold with his friend's handkerchief.

"Behind you. They've both been coached. Now remember, Torresdale, and mind Humboldt. He's crazy because you beat him out at football, and he'll do anything, fair or unfair. You will have to watch him," said Smith, earnestly.

"I'm not afraid," answered Torresdale, grimly.

The other two men stood waiting. Johnson, the taller, was a loosely-put-together, raw-boned countryman, fresh from the lumber regions of northern New York. He had been used to handling logs and men all his life, and his outdoor work had made his muscles like wire cords and his lungs like bellows. Yielding to persuasion, he had worn his room-mate's football suit, and now stood looking down at the padded trousers, grinning at the figure he cut. To him the prospect of a rush was amusing. Until now, his fights had been with drunken Irishmen and bearded Swedes in the lumber camps. This seemed as if it might be tame, and he did not anticipate much difficulty in doing his share toward holding the flag.

H. Lockwood (H. to distinguish him from his brother, of the same class) was of a different type. His build was short and stocky, with a huge chest and broad shoulders, and the even development of the muscles in his arms and forearms, visible beneath the sleeves of his jersey, showed the unmistakable signs of gymnastic training. Lockwood had come to college holding the amateur championship in boxing

and wrestling of three Eastern States; but as
he stood by his classmate's side, and looked at
the crowd in front, and the crowd behind him,
he gave the belt of his corduroys another pull,
for he had heard of and seen some college rushes,
and he did not feel as confident as Johnson.

Torresdale bent down to catch Billy Smith's
farewell injunctions, and, turning, walked over
to join the others. He was not afraid, but his
heart was beating fast as he looked across the
clear space, and saw the three strapping sophomores who were to be their opponents, loung-
ing confidently, and idly listening to a couple
of seniors with an air which plainly showed
that they felt no nervousness as to the combat's
outcome. H. Lockwood seemed to feel the
same way, for, as he greeted Torresdale, he said,
"How are you, Torresdale," and then, nodding
toward the group, "Husky-looking beggars,
are n't they?" Johnson simply said, "Hello
there, Football; how do you like my clothes?"
and shook hands; but each knew that no matter
what the others felt or thought, they were going

to hang on to that flag, if it were a possible thing, though their fingers should be fairly pulled off their hands.

"Mind what I told you, Johnson. And you, too, H. Lockwood. Watch for that underhold," cried Billy Smith, as he went off to find the captain of the team, who was to start the rush.

The men nodded, and through nervousness Torresdale nodded with them. Lockwood wiped the perspiration from his hands on his jersey, and said, between his teeth, "I wish we were ready. I don't like this standing still." Torresdale nodded again in sympathy. Big Johnson grinned, and said, "Lots of time, boys, — lots of time."

Little Tyler, who at first tried desperately to keep pace with Torresdale as he ran in response to the junior's call, had fallen behind, and now hung around the outskirts of the crowd, watching eagerly everything that took place. His heart was banging and thumping in a most startling manner; but in his excitement he did not feel it. He noticed the group of sophomores, around their chosen men, put their heads together and hold a whispered consultation; and one of the men in the middle of the ring seemed to be explaining something. He caught the words, "This way," and "They'll have to let go," and he edged nearer, hoping to discover something that would be of value to his class. As he drew near, one of the sophomores saw him, and yelled, "Get out of this, you dash little fool!"

"You come and put me out!" cried Little Tyler, bravely; but the sophomore only laughed, and said, "Go on home. We don't want to hurt you."

Little Tyler turned away with a sinking heart. "They won't even touch me," he said to himself, bitterly. "Oh, if I could only do something! If they would only give me a chance. But they won't; they won't even touch me. What's the use?"

He walked across the road again, and climbed to the top of a tree-box. He could see over the heads of the crowd there, and, at least, he would be in no one's way. Maybe — just maybe — during the rush he could help in some little way or other. He might see some move that the sophomores were making, and he might warn his class in time, or something like that. It was very vague, but he felt it best to stay where he was — for the present, at all events. So he tucked his feet between two of the crossbars of the tree-box, and sat there waiting, a little ball of humanity, with a fluttering pulse.

Suddenly the busy humming of the voices of the crowd ceased. Every one took a deep, full breath, and braced himself. The seniors and juniors drew back from the centre of the open path between the two classes, and held them in check as the captain of the team walked out into the moonlight, carrying the canvas flag. He stood a moment, looking at the two crowds, then, "Bring out your men," he said.

The three sophomores gave their belts a final hitch, and walked out to the centre, wiping their hands on their trousers; Billy Smith led the three freshmen forward. The captain of the team took their hands and placed them, one by one, on the flag. Then he took the hands of the three sophomores in the same way, and placed them so that they alternated, freshman, sophomore, freshman, sophomore, to the last man. Then he stood back.

"Are you ready?" he asked slowly.

Twelve feet planted themselves solidly, and six pairs of eyes glared across the flag at each other. The leaves on the trees lay quiet, and the electric light on the corner ceased its sizzling. Every one held his breath; and Little Tyler, on the tree-box, leaned forward, with his mouth open and his eyes staring.

"Go!"

At the word, the three sophomores gave a sudden, simultaneous jerk, combining all their strength. The freshmen stumbled, lost their footing, regained it, and the crowds behind them swept together with a mighty yell. The rush had begun.

In the very first struggle H. Lockwood, falling forward with the rest, doubled the hand that he had stretched out to break his fall, backwards beneath him, spraining his wrist badly. The sudden pain that went shooting up his arm convinced him that something serious had happened; but his face gave no sign of any mishap, and it was not until he found the grip of his right hand powerless that he realized what had occurred. Then his heart sank. He knew that another jerk like the first would break his one-handed hold, and unless help came before then the odds of three to two would probably prove fatal. He braced his feet, and hung on doggedly; but it was as he had expected. With a sudden, quick movement the sophomores turned, and in some way caught the end of the flag over Humboldt's shoulder. Then they braced, and with pulls and jerks slowly raised the three struggling freshmen clear from the ground. The crowd yelled, and Lockwood felt his grip slowly loosening under the strain. In a few year-seeming seconds he would have to let go, and the sophomores, who had seen his injured hand hanging loosely by his side, redoubled their efforts. Torresdale and Johnson, their eyes almost starting from their sockets under the strain, dug their heels anew into the chopped-up ground, and hung on grimly. Then, just at the needed moment, the classes clashed together, and a dozen eager and willing freshmen hands laid hold and helped.

With the meeting of the crowds the character of the struggle changed. All individuality ceased, and the rush became entirely class against class. As a whole, it was good-natured; but the feeling that prompted it in the beginning ran high in spots, and here and there little swirling mêlées broke out, although, in the main, the object was the flag, and no one paid much attention to individual fights.

The sophomores pulled, and tugged, and twisted, and the freshmen tugged, and twisted, and pulled. The balance of the sophomores on the outside swung around in a half circle, and savagely attempted to force the freshmen down Buffalo Hill. The freshmen, seeing the trick, swung around also, and the positions of the two classes were reversed. Then the freshmen became savage, and with many howls tried to force their opponents down Eddy Street. They pushed, and panted, and fought; but the sophomores, in spite of all their efforts, did not budge. The crowd on the inside struggled and grappled, and clambered over one another in their efforts to break the hold of the different champions and wrench the flag free. As fast as a sophomore would climb upon a freshman's back to reach the bit of canvas, two freshmen would seize him by the throat and drag him backwards. Whenever a freshman would essay to duck under a man's arm to get nearer, two or three sophomores would grab him by the heels and dump him on his face on the ground, whence, as soon as he was free from the entangling feet, he would spring up to try it all over again. The classes rapidly became mixed. There was soon no freshman or sophomore side: nothing but one large, pushing, kicking, gasping lot of men, all trying to reach the centre of the crowd, where a handful of the more fortunate battled for the possession of the coveted piece of canvas.

For fully thirty minutes the struggle raged without a check. Men who had never trained, and often some who were in the pink of condition, after fighting for fifteen or twenty minutes, came staggering out of the mass, reeling like drunken men, so fierce was the fight. They rested for five or ten minutes, and rushed back with all their old. enthusiasm. Along the edges, the upper-classmen lounged, urging on their favorite classes with: "Get in there, Ninety Dash!" or "Eat 'em up, Ninety Blank!" One group of juniors, standing closer in than the rest, pounced on the resting freshmen as they made ready to renew the conflict, and catching them by the arms and legs tossed them high over the heads of the crowd, on whom they fell with telling force, bowling over sophomores and freshmen impartially, and causing no end of fun to the group of townies on the fence.

Little Tyler almost fell from his tree-box in his anxiety to get a better view. He had seen H. Lockwood let go, and he had groaned. He had seen the rushing freshmen reach the flag in time, and he had laughed. Now, as he saw the group of juniors, he was seriously contemplating climbing down and requesting them to toss him also. If he had thought that he could have done the slightest good, he would not have hesitated an instant, for from where he sat he could see that his class was not having the easy time Torresdale had predicted. Indeed, they were scarcely holding their own.

As the tussle went on, the sophomores had, unnoticed by the freshmen, been gradually massing themselves together. Little Tyler, whom no move escaped, saw it, and, fearful lest his class should be surprised, cried out at the top of his thin, high voice, "Look out for a rush, Ninety Dash!" The butcher, standing beneath the tree, looked up at him curiously. No one else had heard, and, in a despairing sort of way, he settled back again on the tree-box to watch.

But this time there was going to be no sudden rush and attempt to force the freshmen over the hill. The sophomores were after that flag, and the scheme, part of which Little Tyler had overheard, before the rush began, was approaching its fulfilment. More cries of "This way, Ninety Blank!" and "Get together, fellows!" brought a perfect division of parties. The dozen men nearest the flag still clung desperately together, though of the freshmen holders there remained only Torresdale. The other places were filled by men who had fought their way in. Johnson and Lockwood were still in the thick of the trouble, but each had lost his hold, in some of the twistings and turnings of the rush, and was now trying to regain it. Dickson, of the sophomores, had become completely winded in the earlier stages, and now sat, disconsolate and unnoticed, on the hillside; while Birdsell and Humboldt fought weakly to regain their old positions.

Suddenly the sophomores around the inner circle drew to one side, still keeping their hold

on the flag; and before the look of perplexed
wonder at this strange move had died from the
freshman's eyes the others fell back, and up the
path thus made, eleven of the very biggest of
the sophomores came rushing, formed in a perfect and terrible football wedge.

Little Tyler turned faint with fear, and for
a moment held tightly to the tree-box. As
the solid mass of men broke through the ring
and fell upon the startled freshmen, he saw
Humboldt drop his hold and jump savagely,
knee forward, full at Torresdale's chest. The
big guard struck out blindly, and went down
like a ninepin; and all but one of his classmates,
forced to loose their hold under the furious
onslaught, were pushed, staggering, back among
their fellows.

Then Little Tyler became delirious. The
next thing he saw was that a sophomore, watching his chance in the mixup, had, by a quick
movement, jerked the flag from the hands of its
last defender, and was racing madly through the
crowd, with the evident intention and desire of

getting free with his booty. The freshmen saw him, and with him their only chance of turning defeat into victory, vanishing into the distance, and with a disappointed yell they turned and started in pursuit.

But the sophomore was fast, and had a good start, and he chuckled as he ran, forgetting the old, old proverb of the premature crow. There was no one in his path. His course was clear to victory and fame — save for two small obstacles: Little Tyler and his class spirit, both more formidable than any one had ever dreamed.

Before the sophomore was fairly on his way, the hunchback had slid to the ground. He saw that if his enemy held a straight course he must pass within fifteen feet of where he stood. So he hid behind the tree-box and waited. *This* was his chance! It had come, and, oh! he *must* not fail. He would show them now! He would show them! He would show them! — and just then the sophomore came. Little Tyler leaped out from behind the tree, his little legs

8 113

flying back and forth like the driving rods
on an engine. The sophomore saw him and
swerved, but not soon enough. Little Tyler
was too close, by the fraction of a second, and
the little bent-up body shot through the air
like an arrow, the long arms wound themselves
tightly around the sophomore's legs, just above
the knees, and the enemy fell heavily, — a vic-
tim to a prettier tackle than was ever seen on a
Cornell football field. As they lay together,
the butcher, who had retreated in dismay to his
shop-door, saw Little Tyler's hand reach out
and pick up a piece of canvas that the sophomore had dropped in his fall. He wondered
what it all meant. He was still wondering,
when the crowd of freshmen swept up and
surrounded the pair with an unassailable circle,
ten deep. The rush was won.

When Little Tyler opened his eyes, he was
in the centre of a vast crowd of friendly faces.
The air was splitting with howls and cheers.
Men were dancing in each other's arms and
yelling their lungs out, and above the most

frantic of all the cries the name of Tyler crashed with a yell that set the window-panes of the corner grocery rattling with fright. The men were going wild with joy, and, what was more surprising, the sophomores themselves were booming out their own class yell, and following it with his name. Some one yelled, "What's the matter with Tyler?" and the crowd came back with a bellowing, "He's all right!" that woke the sleeping echoes on the hillside and sent the fishes of Cayuga trembling to deeper water. Men of his class whom he had never even seen before climbed over each other's backs to grasp his hand. A crowd of the more thoughtless wanted to throw him on their shoulders. Juniors and seniors with moustaches came up to congratulate him, and his brain whirled and his sight dimmed from the confusion and strangeness of it all.

Then he understood. Then the fulness of it came over him, and he knew what it all meant. He knew that the flag and the rush were not the only things he had won. He knew that there would be no more ignoring, no more leaving him out, — no more suspicion of his cowardice or lack of class spirit. All would be different. He would be in full fellowship, and, as he realized how much it all was to him, his heart fairly stood still for joy. What would that pain in his back ever amount to now? He could stand it were it twice — no, three times as bad. He had shown them. Now they knew. Now they believed. And they were yelling for — for *him*. *For* — *him* — *!*

.   .   .   .

Torresdale knelt beside him, stanching the blood from a cut in his forehead with a sophomore's handkerchief, when the captain of the team pushed his way through the crowd.

"Tyler," said he, in his same deep, heavy voice, "that was the nerviest tackle I have ever seen. Where did you learn it?"

Torresdale bent down to his ear.

"Little Tyler, old man," said he, "do you know that you have saved your class?"

Little Tyler looked up in their faces, started to speak — and then clasped the soiled, ragged bit of canvas more closely to his breast.

"There's class spirit for you, Torry!" said the captain of the team.

"That's not all, Pop," said Torresdale.

COMPANY D'S REVENGE

COMPANY D'S REVENGE

Drill to-morrow afternoon will be at the usual time; all officers and non-commissioned officers should be posted in Company Drill from par to par. The captains of all companies will report to me before drill, and receive instructions for the sham-battle, to be fought on next Tuesday. Companies will line up as follows :

A	B	C	D
E	F	G	H

WOLSEY R. BRAINARD, *Commandant.*

THE next morning D Company, of the First Battalion, was angry.

Now at Cornell, drill, though a trifle below the standard set at West Point, is no idle dream. With the exception of physical wrecks, athletes, law-school men, and co-eds, every one in all the university must grind for four solid terms at the manual and marching movements. If a man, no matter who, snaps his fingers insolently in the face of the university, and loudly denounces the grind, saying that he came to college to

121

study, and not to be a tin soldier, he is more than likely to find at the end of his four years that his cards in the Registrar's office are marked, 1 Drill 0 and 2 Drill 0, which means that the university politely, but firmly, refuses to graduate him. This is, of course, a nuisance. On the other hand, if a man drills quietly, and without making a fuss, the university is so grateful that it allows him three cuts each term, and a leniency touching the matter of sick excuses; and after two years of drill he is given, as a reward, the right to demand a commission, and to become a lieutenant with white stripes on his trousers. Some men ask for their commissions because they are anxious to taste authority, and some because they genuinely like to drill. Most of them, however, sell their uniforms to freshmen, and consider themselves lucky. This commission is freely given, that the companies may have upper-class officers.

In the fall term of each year, there are always a great many freshmen wandering around untied, who have never drilled, and who, consequently, carry arms with the trigger in, and order with one hand over the muzzle. These, and many other things, must be corrected; so the junior and senior officers, and the ambitious sophomores who are competing for "non-coms," take squads of such people and teach them their setting-up exercises, facings, manual and marching movements. Generally, after they have gone through three squad drills, they are sure of their own perfection, and want immediate assignments to the older companies. In time, some are transferred, and the rest are shuffled and cut once, that there may be no unfairness, and divided into four companies. This forms the second battalion. After this, they learn company drill, and frequently execute fours right and fours left at the same time, and sulkily blame their officers for the confusion. Later in the year, they learn better, and are taken up in front of Sage, or across the road from the armory; and sometimes, when the band makes fearfully-constructed discords in the ball cage, they try to keep step jerkily.

At the end of the fall term, they manage to make a fairly decent showing; in the winter they talk about it; and when the spring comes, they entirely forget that the first battalion has had sixteen months more experience, and they become quite arrogant and cocky, which is usually the beginning of their downfall. I know of but one cocky freshman who succeeded, and he was "busted" at the end of his first term. He only carried ten hours, and flunked in English 1 under Krunts, — though that has n't anything to do with this story.

Now in the spring term of every year there is a sham-battle. This is the only thing worth drilling for, and is quite exciting. Townspeople, co-eds, and professors stand and watch it with their fingers in their ears; while hordes of students madly fire blank cartridges at each other, and die at appointed places, — generally where a lucky friend who does not have to drill is waiting with a drink, for it is hard work. It is quite like a regular battle. Officers in slouch hats and leggings ride around the field, gal-

lantly waving edgeless swords, and yelling
hoarse orders that no one hears. Men lie flat
on their stomachs, and aim at the whites of
each other's eyes. The band plays; the artillery
roars; and there are charges and counter-charges
galore. After every one is quite tired, some
of the captains and majors and the colonel get
together behind a stump and consult their pro-
grammes and the library clock, to see if it is
time to do anything more, — to charge, or retreat, or anything. If it is, they go and do it
very fiercely; if it is not, they also go and do it
very fiercely, — so that either way every one is
satisfied.

It is customary in this engagement that the
newer companies shall be defeated. This precedent had been established years before in the
days of the first sham-battle, for it was good
that the under-classes should be kept down. It
is now an upper-class right, along with frock
coats, high hats, and the upper-class table at
Pat's. As it had passed unscathed through
the rigid rule inspection of three detached army

lieutenants, it had become fully recognized by
the university, and not even the defeated under-
classes thought of questioning its absolute just-
ness. This itself is a great deal.

But the coming of Lieutenant Brainard,
U. S. A., and the cockiness of Company F, had
this year turned things upside down, and the
whole university was staring and laughing.
The battle was scheduled for the following
Tuesday, and D Company, the flower of the
whole regiment, had been chosen to be among
the attacking forces, and to be disgracefully
repulsed, with loss. The blow had fallen suddenly, and for a while men's minds were not
thinking. That D Company, whose drill was
a thing to watch, and whose rank and file were
almost, to a man, busted upper-classmen, should
be called upon to suffer ignominious defeat at
the hands of Company F, a mob of half-drilled,
undisciplined sophomores and freshmen commanded by a farmer from the Agricultural
School, was unheard of, and a double insult to
tradition and D Company. Men at first went

around with dazed smiles and uncertain looks, not knowing what would happen next. Then there came a revulsion of feeling; and though the upper-classes felt insulted, they were ready to laugh at D, in case defeat should come. This is the way men do sometimes. F was already laughing.

That the order would not be recalled, all well knew, for Brainard was a martinet, and suffered no protests. There was no relief. On Tuesday afternoon they should be disgraced. Wednesday morning the tale would be in every one's mouth. By Thursday it would be history, and Friday night beer would be bought.

In a hopeless way Fordyce, the captain, had called on the commandant and asked that they might be spared. He pointed out that D Company were older men who, though compelled to drill by an unfeeling university, should not, in his humble opinion, be subjected to further humiliation. He expatiated on the general good behavior of the men, and said that all felt very strongly about it, and that he thought, with all deference to the commandant, that the corps, as a whole, would make a much better showing if D Company should exchange positions with another of the line companies, or even with Company F. Lieutenant Brainard, U. S. A., showed his teeth, and asked questions. Then he said, sternly, that under no conditions would the order or position of companies be changed; and Fordyce came back to his men and said, bitterly, that they were all fools not to have drilled in their first two years, and that he hoped now that some of them who had been coming to drill with tan shoes, no gloves, and some other fellow's trousers, would see what they had done for the company and for him. He was very sarcastic, and the men listened meekly, with eyes correctly to the front, until he gave a savage, "Sergeant, dismiss the company!" and walked away. Then every one ran for the gunracks without waiting for the command, for Puggy Workman was first sergeant, and he never used to say anything but, "Skip, fellows," as soon as Fordyce's back was turned.

Since things are as they are, it is not remarkable that upper-class privates hold themselves far above their rank companions of lesser college age, nor is it strange that D Company should feel insulted.

The men reasoned thus: We have four years in which to complete our two years of drill. We have a right to choose in which two of those years we shall drill. We have chosen; and because we have merely exercised our right, it is rubbed into us by a cheap-skate army lieutenant.

It was no wonder the men were angry, and lingered in groups, discussing ways and means of avoiding the affront to their customs, their company, and themselves. It was no wonder that the ill-concealed smiles of Company F, and the open guying of a lot of law-school men, set the stragglers of Company D, who were pouring singly, and in twos and threes, through the gym. door, wild with an insatiable desire for revenge. D Company did not deserve it; their behavior had been exemplary, their marching worth watching. Their fours were complete at almost every drill. Their officers were efficient. Fordyce had been six years at Shattuck before entering college. Allerton had been a sergeant in the Pennsylvania National Guards. Bug Fulton had ranked them all at one time, but, being too lazy to work, had fallen to his first lieutenancy. Puggy Workman, Monk Cuthbert, Blake, and Johnson were the sergeants, and all the rest were picked from the cream of the unfortunates who had not drilled in their first two years. Moreover, they were all representative men, holding honors among their classmates. Fordyce was Senior President; Allerton was Sigma Xi; Bug Fulton was Senior Toast-master; and Puggy and Tommy Easton were on the Junior Ball Committee. There were few among them whose popularity could not stand alone.

. . . .

Puggy and Johnson, hot with wrath and glum with impotency, were strolling arm in arm to dinner. The chimes were ringing softly; the spring twilight was touching all the earth with restfulness; low over the lake hung just the faintest suggestion of a pointed, silvery moon, — and Puggy and Johnson were angry.

"I can't understand it," Johnson was saying earnestly. "Why should Company D, of all companies, be singled out for this insult? What is Brainard's game? He ought to know enough about the men in D to know that they won't stand it."

"It's easy enough," explained Puggy, bitterly. "It isn't Brainard as much as it is Sawyer and his gang of babies. Sawyer didn't like the idea of his dear freshmen being beaten, so he has gone to Brainard. Now, Brainard's on crutches, and F think they have a good thing in us. We've got to do something. If we let ourselves be calmly pushed aside for under-classes, there won't be any living with them. It's bad enough as it is."

"The trouble is," said Johnson, "that we can't disregard orders and charge F anyway, and

Brainard knows it. A year ago we could have done that. Now we have too many graduations at stake."

"You 're right," admitted Puggy, gloomily; "but something must be done."

"It will," replied Johnson, confidently. "Did you ever know our crowd of fellows to let themselves be run over?"

"We might kill Brainard," suggested Puggy, savagely, "or we might thumbstring Sawyer."

"And we might be idiots," smiled Johnson, sourly, "but we are not. Talk sense, or shut up."

"Who is that on the bridge throwing stones?" asked Puggy.

Johnson looked up. "Blake and Tommy Easton," he replied, after a moment. "Wonder where they were!"

"They were n't at drill."

"No, I noticed. Yeaa, Tommy! Yeaa, Blake!"

The figures on the bridge waved their hands and resumed their target practice. As Johnson and Puggy approached, Blake staggered to the railing with a stone half as large as his head, heaved it over with a grunt, and peered eagerly after it. "Smashed it that time, Tom," he said. "Gosh, look at the hole! Hello, fellows, did you see that shot?"

"Darn your shots," said Johnson. "What do you think of the situation?"

"Don't know what you are talking about," replied Blake; "but both you lads look as though you had been struck in the face with melons. Who's dead?"

"Haven't you heard?" gasped Puggy; "where were you two fellows to-day?"

"Cut," said Tommy, briefly. "Elmira, last night. Awful time. You don't happen to have any ice water in your pocket, do you?"

Then Puggy explained, with Johnson at his back to help him. As the tale was unfolded, Blake and Tommy swore picturesquely.

"But won't Brainard change it?" asked Tommy.

"You might ask him," said Johnson, witheringly. "Jack Fordyce jollied him for over half an hour to-day, while Bug Fulton took the Company. I believe Brainard told him · to go to thunder, or something like that."

"Jack's all cut up about it, too," added Puggy. "He came back and called us all fools, and nearly bit my head off when he told me to dismiss."

"Well, I don't blame him," replied Blake, warmly. "Jack Fordyce has worked hard enough over our gang of loafers; and I, for one, think it a mighty mean trick of Brainard's. Why can't he let things alone, instead of meddling with affairs that don't concern him! By Jove, we won't do it! We *must* do something," and he glowered savagely at a co-ed across the road.

"Let's all get together on it," suggested Johnson. "There are four of us here, and we'll get Bug Fulton."

"Over in your rooms?" asked Blake.

"No, yours. I've a freshman."

"All right, here's Bug now. Hi, Bug!"

Robert Quarrier Fulton, commonly known by the somewhat less elegant, but shorter name of Bug, came across the street, savagely kicking up all the dust within his reach. One could see that his temper was ruffled. He was a tall, raw-boned Kentuckian, with an unreproducible accent.

"You fellows are dandies, I must say," he said contemptuously. "What do you want?"

"We want you, you skinny Whiskian," said Blake, soothingly. "We want you and your absolutely unswerving support in a time of need. We are going to get out of this hole. Are you in? It may mean trouble."

"Am I in?" said Bug, scornfully, though with glee in his eyes at the possibility of a fight. "Ask me? What is it?"

"We don't know yet," answered Blake. "Fellows here are coming to my rooms to-night and think. Be there. I'm going to eat. So long, fellows. Come on, Johnson!" Blake had a way of breaking off a conversation very abruptly when he was tired, and no one thought anything about it as he and Johnson sauntered away. Only Puggy yelled after him, "We'll be there. Half-past seven!" and Blake waved his hand, without turning around to show that they had heard.

The four remained leaning over the railing and talking until the big bell on the campus struck half-past six. Then they bent their backs and walked on up the hill.

At dinner they met Torresdale, who had never drilled, having always been excused on account of football and crew work. He laughed as they came in. "How well trained are you for your run Tuesday?" he asked.

"Never *you* mind," said Bug. "You're not doing it."

"I can see your finish, Puggy," continued Torresdale, teasingly. "Any one with your wind, too!"

"See here, you great big, good-looking thing!" said Puggy, good-naturedly, "I'll bet you sodas we take that artillery."

"Crowd?" asked Torresdale.

"No, you and I."

"Done," said Torresdale, and the two shook hands.

"You 're just that much poorer, Torresdale," said Tommy. "Want to do it again?"

"Thanks, but I don't care to write home for more money. That would break me if I lost. Wait till next Tuesday. You 'll see," and he clattered up the stairs, chuckling. A minute later his classmates heard him howling, "Who wants to bat out fliyies? Ay, there, Billy Wilbur, come ahead!"

Shortly afterwards the three fellows heaved simultaneous sighs, and rose heavily with lighted pipes. On their way to Blake's rooms they met the Freshman who boarded at Cascadilla. The Freshman had been at a military prep. school, and on account of his excellence in drill there attained had been honored by membership in Company D. When he heard what was up, he eagerly joined the party, and four strong they swept in on Blake.

For a long time they sat and smoked and

thought with wrinkled foreheads. Scheme after scheme was evolved and cast aside. Daring plots were made to steal Brainard, even as they once had stolen a freshman toastmaster. The Freshman was for putting jalap in Company F's food. This was extremely freshmanish, besides being impracticable. Puggy wanted to hire a lot of townies and muckers to shell the enemy with stones. Blake was anxious to adopt the Chinese mode of fighting, by having three or four men throw assafœtida and other ill-smelling things from the library tower. Tommy, in despair, thought it best to charge, and, when the arraignment for disobedience came, to pretend the orders had been misunderstood. They had almost reached the end of their rope, and had settled down to the clenched-teeth, by-Jove-we-will-find-a-scheme way of thinking before there were any results. Now every one knows that for results this is the best stage one can possibly attain, and ten minutes had not passed before Bug Fulton brought his fist down on the table with a bang that meant business, and set the student lamps and the window-panes dancing.

"Whoop!" he yelled, "I 've got it! I 've got it! By Jove, fellows, Company F will be the sickest gang of farmers Tuesday night you ever saw. I — oh — eee — wow — wow," and he went into gale after gale of laughter. In a flash Puggy seized him around the neck, Tommy pulled his feet out, and, as he fell, Blake sat heavily on his head and hammered his back, adjuring him to stop laughing, and tell them. The Freshman smiled uncertainly at this sacrilegious treatment of a senior. Bug gasped and choked. "Let up, Puggy," he gurgled; "you are choking me."

Puggy took his arm away, and Bug went off into another fit of laughter. When they had pounded him again to silence, he sat up weakly, and told his plan; and, truly, it was simple, as he told it. D Company should not only capture the heights, but should also hold them, and their flag should wave victoriously over the enemy's cannon.

It was glorious. No one should get into trouble; no one should disobey orders; and F Company should run like frightened sheep. The battle should go down to subs, sub-subs, and subs yet unborn, as The Stand of The Upper-classmen, and it should show the futility of further foolishness. The name of Company D should ring through the future as the up-holder of precedent and custom. It was certainly glorious.

When the first enthusiasm had worn away, Blake suggested that they take off their coats, fill fresh pipes, and discuss the details of the scheme. Bug, as it was his idea, lawfully assumed command.

"Tommy," said he to Easton, "I want you and Puggy to see and sound every man in D Company before next Friday. Take the roster and go personally to each man. Report to me before drill. You can divide up the work as you choose."

Puggy and Tommy nodded.

Bug went on, "The Freshman must find out

how many men in Company F keep their uniforms in the gym. lockers, and he must also learn the numbers of those lockers. That will not be hard, for most of Company F are in his class. If he needs help, I will detail our other two freshmen to assist him."

"Don't need them," said the Freshman, shortly.

"All right; only be careful. Don't let them get on. Report to me with the lists as soon as you can, for stealing the combinations from Doc. Fitchfield's office won't be any easy job. However, I will do that; and I wish, Johnson, that you would see Fordyce and Allerton, and tell them not to come to drill Friday. There is no use in more than one man's losing his commission. Blake, I want you to make whatever arrangements about the farm that you can. See that the covers are all shut down on Monday night, and be sure that you know the exact location of every box. There is apt to be trouble if you don't, you know," and Bug smiled grimly.

"I'm on," said Blake; "don't worry."

"Every one must have these informations by Friday, at four-forty-five, remember," continued Fulton, impressively, "and there mustn't be a hitch anywhere."

"Gosh, I wouldn't be that jay captain for love," grinned Johnson.

"Thank goodness, it is settled," said the Freshman, timidly; and every one smoked softly for a few minutes. A group of students strolled by under the window, talking, and the five conspirators looked at each other and grinned. The captain and first lieutenant of Company F had been among them. They had heard him laugh, and they were all thinking the same thing. The minutes stole away in smoke clouds. Soon Tommy brought his feet from the table to the floor, and there followed a yawn or two, and a general knocking out of pipes. Then Johnson arose. "I'm sleepier than a lecture on the gas engine," he announced: "come to bed, fellows." The others rose.

"Friday afternoon, then," said Bug, and with

good-nights the four rattled down the stairway, and, locking arms, swung up the street, musically bellowing, —

"One-two, three-four, all fall in line;
To the tune of our Pro-o-fs we'll keep strict in time;"

while Blake, not to be outdone, roared defiance through a tin horn, as he leaned far out of the window.

When on the following Friday the last call was sounded, and Puggy Workman, resplendent in new cotton gloves and a real shirt, barked a gruff, "Company D, fall in! Right shoulder — grwow!" there was not one man on the company's roster whose piece did not come ringing to the order as his name was called. Only Fordyce and Allerton were missing, and Bug reported to the commandant and took charge. Puggy and Tommy had done their work well.

Company F had not yet formed. Their officers were late, as usual; and, as D rattled by them at double time, they were greeted by howls of derision.

"Getting in practice for Tuesday?" yelled a freshman.

"You little fool," said Cuthbert, in his throat, "your skin won't be so white by Tuesday night," and they swept on savagely. In a moment they had turned into Central Avenue, and a "Column half right" and a "Quick time, march," ringing from the front, faced them toward the campus, at a long swinging step. Bug was taking them back of the library to the field of the following Tuesday's engagement. Bug was foxy, and well knew the value of his step. The criminal who sees his gallows realizes more thoroughly his coming disgrace.

There would not be much drill for D Company this day. There was too much to be said and decided. Outside of the conspirators, none of the men knew what was up, further than that their reputations were in some way to be saved.

Bug Fulton, marching by Puggy's side, chuckled, as he turned and said, "That freshman and the rest of F did us a good turn down by the armory. Some of the men need to be just a little madder."

"We'll get up another small demonstration, just to clinch things, when we go back," replied Puggy, out of the corner of his mouth.

"Right!" said Bug. "Guide is *left*, men! Blake says the boxes are all right. Twelve of them — all full."

"Holy smoke!" grinned Puggy, as his imagination worked.

"Fordyce and Allerton never said a word either. They are all right."

"Are they on?"

"To some extent, of course; but — s-s-steady! No talking in ranks!" for the men were getting impatient.

"How about the Kid?" asked Puggy, after saying Hip-Hip-Hip for a few minutes.

"Got 'em all except two. He's a good freshman."

"And you?"

"Sunday — can't do it on week days. Flannigan's there. Here we are. Column *right*.

Haah!" and the file turned at right angles across the grass between Morrill and McGraw. They went a few rods further, into the shade of some trees, and then fours right, halt, and rest followed each other rapidly. The men sat and sprawled over the green grass and waited for news. Bug let them wait until he believed every man as he would have him. Then he began speaking.

"Men," he said, "you all know the orders that Lieutenant Brainard has seen fit to give concerning this term's sham-battle. You all know by this time that we, Company D, of the First Battalion, and almost all upper-classmen, have been chosen to bear the disgrace of being the first old company in the history of Cornell to be defeated by a lot of freshmen and farmers. Let me point out to you our places next Tuesday. Company F holds the keystone position, — there, yonder, in that row of trees and bushes on the hill. Two of the other defensive companies flank F on either side, with one as a reserve in the rear. A, B, C, and D are

146

down in the hollow, just behind the library. We are to advance by companies, and *we* hold the colors. A and B charge G and H; E, the reserve, charges to meet B; but C comes in on their left flank, and stops their game. Then E, G, and H are to surrender. We, the color company, and the best of the lot, have orders to charge and be disgracefully beaten, losing over three-quarters of our men, and finally giving up our arms and colors to a gang of freshies, sophs, and farmers commanded by a yahoo whose main study here has been 'Jones on Manure.' Have you heard the jeers and gibes that Company F have been throwing at us ever since the orders went out? Have you heard that Brown, their first sergeant, told Jack Fordyce, who has worked like a horse over this company, and who is all broke up over this business, that he ought to be *glad* the defence was held by F, as his set of muckers did n't know how to hold a gun yet? Have you heard that Porter, another of their hay-gatherers, told Allerton that all we were good for was breaking stone? [Bug had not heard any of these things, but he knew his business.] Did you hear them horse us as we passed to-day?

"Now the question is, shall we or shall we not submit to Lieutenant Brainard's stepping in here, fresh from West Point, and upsetting our old and settled customs? Shall we let our colors and our company become the sport of the whole college? If you say yes, well and good; but your officers will be ashamed of you. If you say no, I will show you a way in which you can, without disobeying one single order, or losing any chance of graduating, completely annihilate Company F, and stand victorious and avenged on the top of that hill. *Company D, attention!*" The men scrambled to their feet, and stood like statues. Then Bug's voice rang out again over the two flushed and eager lines. "I want every man who will stand by Jack Fordyce and D Company to advance two paces."

The two lines took a deep, savage breath, swayed, and, as one man, stepped twice forward. Bug and Puggy beamed, and the former's voice, husky with loud speaking, still rang triumphantly as he thanked the men.

"Now," Bug went on more coolly, "I want to tell you the scheme. The sergeant will call the roll again, and I want each man to answer to his name, and state the number of cuts he has had this term."

The call commenced, and from Allen to Zimmerman, but three men had taken their allowance. These were Blake, Tommy Easton, and Puggy.

"Now, men, the idea is this," began Bug again. "You are each allowed three cuts. That right is yours, and is inalienable. You can take them when you wish, and — there are only *three of you who need drill next Tuesday.* I — " but the men had caught the idea, and, despite all discipline, a yell went up from the ranks that Company E, half a mile away, heard and wondered at. Men laughed and danced, and flung their hats in the air, for it had been a terribly narrow escape. Some private proposed three cheers for Fulton, and fifty strong young voices roared, "Hip-Yeaaa!" three times, with a Fulton at the end loud enough to shake the library windows. Bug blushed, and Puggy smiled benevolently. Cheers followed for Fordyce, and Allerton, and Company D. Then they started on the non-coms and privates, and would probably have been yelling yet, if Puggy had not reminded Bug that Brainard would probably be out on the war path if it was not stopped. Bug wiped the perspiration from his face, and brought them, grinning, to attention. Then he commanded silence, very sternly, and the men twisted their faces straight. Only here and there, in the quiet following noise, the sounds a man makes when he laughs out and stops suddenly popped all along the lines like the last firecrackers in a bunch. In a few moments there was silence again, and Bug continued: —

"There are some further details in this scheme, by which we hope to teach Company F a lesson, and place them where they belong.

We want volunteers." Without waiting for the word, the whole company stepped two paces forward, laughing.

"I 'm sorry," observed Bug, "that we can't use you all. Thirty men is all we shall need, — I should like to have those men, and only those, who are *particularly* anxious to serve."

Again the company trailed arms and advanced two paces. This was contagious, and Bug grinned.

"Take them all, and divide them up," whispered Puggy; so Bug did, and detailed ten to the Freshman, twenty to Blake, and kept twenty. He explained to them that they were to follow their leaders implicitly, and that the reason a freshman had been placed in charge of one detachment was that he knew the details of the plans, and had already partially worked one of them out. No one demurred. This is one advantage of being a good freshman. It was arranged that the first detachment should report to the Freshman at ten o'clock, Monday night, in the gully back of the engine-room.

The Freshman would tell them what to do when they got there. The second detachment should report to Puggy at the Stewart Avenue entrance to the cemetery. The rest were to meet Bug back of the library. The first line of "Alma Mater" was agreed on as a signal, and it should be answered by the second. They were cautioned not to use any lights, and to make no noise, and, above all, to say absolutely nothing in reply to the sneers of Company F or any one else. This was the hardest thing they had to do, but it was necessary.

People remarked that day on the swing and life that Company D put into their march and manual, as they came down the road at the recall. Lieutenant Brainard saw them, and, as they thundered up South Avenue at double time, turned on the grass, and halted together, with the precision of a veteran company, he bit his lip, and began to wonder a little if he had not made a mistake.

The Colonel of the regiment came up. He was a tall, handsome fellow, with blue eyes and

a brown skin; and, saluting, he asked what that
noise had been up on the campus where Company D had been drilling. Bug returned the
salute, and replied that he believed that Cascadilla played Ithaca High School at baseball up
there somewhere. Then the Colonel saluted,
and Bug saluted, and the Colonel went away.

The other companies were coming in at double
time, turning, obliquing, and taking their old
positions. Hoarse commands followed each
other in rapid succession, and the ring of the
pieces coming to order mingled with the rattle
of the bayonets fixing. Finally, all was quiet,
and Lieutenant Wolsey R. Brainard, U. S. A.,
and Commandant of the Cornell University
Corps of Cadets, stepped forth, flanked by the
Colonel and the Adjutant, and made his formal
announcement of the coming battle. It was a
long thing, starting with, "Atten*tion !* " and
ending with, "Dismi*ss* your companies; " and
while it was being given Company D glared
across the grass into the face of Company F,
and Lieutenant Fulton, standing stiffly in front

of his own command, winked solemnly at its captain, Sawyer. Company F and Captain Sawyer smiled amiably, but with concealed malice; and by the time this was done, the rest of the two battalions were madly shouting, whooping, yelling, and struggling in a white-helmeted, cartridge-belted, bayoneted mass at the side-door of the armory. Five minutes more, and Bug, Puggy, Tommy, Blake, Johnson, Cuthbert, and the Freshman were tearing dinner-wards with surprising speed and spirit.

.   .   .   .

If any one had chanced to pass along the car tracks, just behind the university engine-house, at about ten o'clock on the evening of May 19, 189-, and if any one had stopped and listened very intently, a few subdued voices might have been heard; but that would have been all. Later, if any one had thought to go quietly to the little ground windows of the bowling alley, they might have seen lights moving here and there, and lockers being softly opened. The

Freshman was doing his duty, and doing it well.

Meanwhile Blake, with twenty men, good and true, was doing a noiseless, double-time across the cemetery and up South Avenue. As they reached East they halted, and were ordered to separate, and proceed singly to the rear of the largest university barn, for a great many professors live on East Avenue, and professors rampant are not good things. In whispers, it was decided that if any man were not there by eleven o'clock he should return, as best he might, to where Bug Fulton and his twenty men should be. If he were lost from all the rest, he should whistle, but only in case he was lost, as the signal might attract attention. Then, in a dead silence, Blake gave the whistle, and Bug Fulton, up behind the library, answered, which meant, " All 's well — hurry."

It had been agreed that three-quarters of an hour after this signal the three forces, with their work accomplished, should meet behind the library and put the finishing touches to their labors. Meanwhile, Bug was to post a double line of sentinels, — one reaching toward the farm, and the other toward the armory, — to keep watch on any stragglers who might be coming up or down the campus at that time of night. Bug himself, with Cuthbert, remained in hiding, back of the library, on the hill that Company F was to occupy the next day. If anything went wrong, or if help was needed, either by the Freshman or by Blake, a report was to be made to the nearest sentinel, who, in turn, should bear it, with all possible haste, to Bug. It had been rumored that Company F had been acting suspiciously, and a surprise was feared.

The two watchers waited in silence. There was no moon, and the night was black as ink. The figure of the first and nearest sentry, which had been dimly outlined against the horizon, was swallowed from view, and even the college buildings looked like indistinct blurs and patches of darker black on black. High up in the physiological lecture-room of McGraw Hall one little light shone forth. The assistant was doubtless correcting examination papers.

Cuthbert turned and looked at the lights of the town and of West Hill. Out on the lake they both heard the chug-chug of a steam canal-boat towing a string of barges to Cayuga. Bug yawned, and, putting his head under Cuthbert's coat, lit his pipe, in direct violation of his own orders. Cuthbert did the same thing, using Bug's coat, and they sat for a long time in absolute silence.

The clock chimed a quarter to eleven; and as the last tones died, they heard the sound of voices far away. "Hark!" whispered Bug, and they listened.

"That can't be Blake; it's too early," said Cuthbert.

Just then a sentry dashed up, out of breath. "Party of men coming up Central Avenue," he gasped. "They refuse the signal." Bug started up.

"Go back and find out who they are, and report at once! Pass the word to the others to keep the strictest lookout. Cuth, go and tell the first of the farm sentries the same thing," said Bug, quickly. "You'll find him at the first door of White. Hurry back!" and the sentry went one way, and Cuthbert another.

Bug, left alone, swore silently, and bit through the stem of his pipe.

Cuthbert returned first. "I told him," he panted; "everything has been quiet up there."

"We didn't imagine any row could come from that side, anyway," mused Bug. "But this Central Avenue gang — you'll have to go over there and investigate, too, Cuth. I'm sorry, but—"

"Wait," said Cuthbert. The first sentry came tumbling back. "It's all right," he puffed, and sat down on the ground. "The Freshman," he added.

"Of course!" said Cuthbert.

Beyond the library the whistle echoed. The sentry answered disjointedly; and ten men, bearing twenty odd-looking bundles, swept, grinning, up the hill.

"You Indian," chuckled Cuthbert, "why the deuce did n't you answer us?"

"Could n't," breathed the Freshman. "We'd just passed Prexy and the Dean. They eyed us."

"What are all those," asked Bug, pointing to the black bundles.

"Uniforms," said the Kid, nonchalantly. "All of them did not keep their belts in the lockers; and I thought it best to make a good job of it."

"You blessed Kid," whispered Bug, hoarsely. "What in the dickens shall we do with them? Throw them down, fellows;" and the twenty uniforms fell in a heap on the grass.

"Looks like an old-clothes store," said Newton.

"We'll have to — Hello!" said Cuthbert. Off to the left a series of whistles was heard and answered, and the next minute a strange procession turned the corner of Morrill. Two by two they came, walking warily, with pale, white faces. Each two carried carefully, between them, a box about two feet square. As they slowly and gingerly picked their way down the hill, and up the other side, the watchers on the summit held their sides in ecstasies of laughter. Blake came first, carrying one box all alone. He stumbled once, and the beads of cold perspiration broke out on his forehead and ran down to his chin. Puggy and Van Cleef followed, looking scared to death, and behind them came the rest, all blue with fright.

"Jove!" said Blake, with twitching lips, "I would n't do that again for money," and he tenderly set down his burden and wiped his brow. The others followed, and every man sighed, with a sigh not wholly of physical relief, and went as far away from it as possible.

"You've no idea," said Puggy. "Seemed as if we carried those dod-gasted things five miles, and not knowing what minute we'd be — Brrr!!" But the other thirty men were rolling with laughter.

"Any one hurt?" Bug asked between gasps.

"Tommy and Ted Witherspoon are running yet, I guess," replied Puggy, mirthfully, now that he was safe. "They dropped their box." The crowd roared.

At last, when things became quiet, Bug picked out places in the bushes where the ten boxes and the uniforms would be safely hidden. Then the sentry detail went to work, for the others would not touch them. After they had all been safely stowed away, they very gently took off the covers. After this every one felt better, and went home quite quickly.

   .   .   .   .

Now a day in summer is notably longer than a day in winter. Whether the hours stretch, or whether there are more of them, has not, I believe, been yet entirely decided, but it is certain that the day following D Company's night raid was longer than most. That is, it was long until drill commenced. After that, there was so much going on and off that the time passed quickly.

At about four o'clock, carriages, filled with people of every sort and variety, began to appear from somewhere and disappear campusward. After these came a horde of townspeople, some in rags, some in tags, and some who doubtless would have been in velvet gowns had it been fashionable at that time. Little muckers, eager to see the fight, crowded pompous old ladies and gentlemen who were anxious to view the evolutions. Young girls, with eyes fairly dancing with excitement, chattered among themselves or to their escorts, now and again recognizing, with many hurried remarks to their neighbors, the face of an officer or private among the men strolling from the different fraternity houses to the armory. Groups of students in red sweaters and pipes mixed here and there, and were fearfully admired and imitated at a distance by a group of Cascadilla school-boys. A crowd of seniors who did not like noise, and so would not go to the sham-battle, were knocking out flies on the green just west of the gym. and yelling,

"Let it go—" "That's mine," "I—yi! Pull 'em out the ether!" and many other remarks of a similar nature. Out in the middle of the dusty road, two dogs were playfully snapping at each other. It was easy to see that the battle would be interesting.

In front of the armory, all was bustle and confusion. There seemed to be some trouble. The artillery was ready to start for the front, but something was delaying its support, Company F. Only about half the company were there, and their captain wore an anxious, worried look as he talked earnestly with his lieutenant. Soon the lieutenant disappeared through the armory door. The artillery grew very impatient, and requested Company F to smoke up. Company F, being nervous, took offence, and things became a little unpleasant for a while. The captain fumed and lost his temper. In a few minutes the lieutenant appeared at the head of twenty wild-looking, dazed, and ununiformed men—the rest of Company F.

"Why, you idiots!" yelled the captain, "where are your uniforms?"

"Some one has stolen them," said a sergeant, sullenly saluting. He did not like to be called names.

"Stolen them!" echoed the captain, scornfully. "Walked right into your lockers and took them out! I don't suppose they minded little things like double combinations. What in the deuce should any one want with your uniforms?"

"They might have been some townies who would have sold them," suggested the lieutenant, cautiously.

The captain turned on him. "You make me tired," he said, "B. Poore himself would n't give five dollars for ten of them. Those men are faking; they are afraid, afraid to buck Company D, who have walked all over us for over a term. Bah! Stolen!" He turned to the troops. "You're good soldiers," he said, "it's a pity you can't drill and have n't any courage. You are —" what else they were

was never said, for word came from the front,
through a panting orderly, that unless Company
F was in position with the artillery within ten
minutes, their place would be forfeited. The
captain savagely ordered the ununiformed men
into the rear rank, and cursed pathetically, as
the motley-looking angry set of freshmen stumbled up the campus in front of the rattling gun
battery. Captain Fordyce and Lieutenants Fulton and Allerton, with the remnants of D Company, were already on the field. Puggy, as first
sergeant, had promptly ordered Blake and Tommy Easton to fall in, and as Bug told Fordyce that he knew positively that the rest of
the men were going to cut, Fordyce smiled and
marched his three musketeers to their position.
Lieutenant Brainard had seen them, and went
to inquire what all this farce meant. Fordyce
looked him straight in the eye, and respectfully
told him that at the last moment he had received
word that the rest of the company proposed to
cut rather than to be humiliated. Brainard
chewed his moustache, and his face grew red

and white by turns. His impotency, and the knowledge that D Company had been too much for him, made him angry, but knowing how necessary it was, to him, that the battle should go off without any hitches or slow scene-changes, he told Fordyce to act as though he had the whole company back of him. He said it was necessary for each company to act as a unit, regardless of numbers. Bug knew this, and had included it in his calculations. Then the commandant went away, and the company grinned. Fordyce was beginning to feel better.

Lieutenant Brainard had just settled down to being thoroughly angry, and had thought of all the cutting things he should have said, when Company F, with its smartly uniformed front rank, and its rag-tag and bob-tail rear, came straggling on the field. A howl of laughter went up from the crowd on the bank as the whole absurdity of the sight struck them. Men from D Company were scattered through the crowd, and took special pains to keep people awake to the humor in the situation. The men in F were blushing.

When Brainard, from the centre of the field, saw all this, through his glasses, he gasped with horror, lost his temper completely, and, walking quickly to F's captain, asked him what this dashed foolishness meant.

"I beg your pardon, sir," said he, hastily saluting, "but the men claim to have lost their uniforms."

"They do, do they?" said Lieutenant Brainard, with his voice trembling, for his heart was hot within him, "then you tell those men to get out of the ranks and hunt for them. Send them home! I won't have them around! You ought to have known better, sir, than to permit such a half-uniformed company to appear on the field. I presumed, when I gave this command to you, that you were competent to hold it. You will report to me in my office to-night, Mr. Sawyer. I shall have something to say to you. Send those men home, and take your position! Are we going to wait for your blundering set of dolts all the afternoon ? *Rear rank, fall out ! Get off the field !* Company, forward — march ! " and as the handful of men moved away shamefacedly, Captain Sawyer, with a face of fiery redness, saluted stiffly. The artillery laughed, and the crowd on the hillside gave, at Johnson's instigation, a rousing farewell jeer.

Truly, it seemed as if D's revenge was complete. F had been held up to ridicule and shame before the whole college and town. The humiliation intended by them for Fordyce and his men had turned as a boomerang, and, hurtling backwards, had fallen with unforeseen effect into their own ranks. It was pitiful, but the worst was yet to come, the men of D remembered.

The battle had begun. Sawyer exhorted his twenty men to retrieve themselves; and the men, with set teeth and rage in their stomachs, smiled fiercely as they thought that, in spite of all, they should hold their position against their persecutors, and that to-morrow their turn would come, when, with twenty inexperienced men they had defeated fifty picked veterans. It was not so bad after all, they said to each other amid the din and smoke. But where *were* those uniforms?

The two twenty-pounders bravely barked defiance from the hill-top, and the battery threw aside their coats for better action. Men darted from gun to caisson, carrying ammunition, and the spongers, dripping with perspiration, gasped as they ran to their guns at each discharge. Along the lines of defence, the officers were pacing, cautioning their commands to keep cool and to wait for the word. Orderlies ran here and there with messages, and peering through the gathering smoke to find their officers. The air was thick with the smell of powder. Only the attacking companies B and C were firing. The others were silent, waiting savagely until they should be closer. Not a wad should be wasted.

Suddenly, far down in the hollows the glint of the afternoon sun struck on an officer's sword, as it flashed from its scabbard, and there went up a mighty roar from the hillside, for Company A was advancing. The men, looking like a mere handful on the plain, ran a little distance over the rough ground and, dropping behind a grassy rise, poured two volleys into Company G, then, rising, ran breathless to the next elevation. There was a deathly silence of ten seconds, and then one long sheet of flame burst with a roar of demons from the bushes on the right. G had broken silence. In the oncoming lines, some staggered and fell, shrieking. The ranks stopped, wavered an instant according to the programme, and swept on. An officer in the rear shouted something in a hoarse voice, and B followed A, firing on the right flank of H as they ran. Men dropped here and there, reeling, for H replied, firing by volleys and doing terrible execution, but the men stumbled on with a cheer until they dropped, breathless, by the side of their comrades of A for shelter. Behind them all, with D Company´and the colors, the band was playing bravely.

D chafed with impatience and eagerness, and

fingered their triggers nervously. The music sent chills of excitement shooting up their spines, and the smell of the smoke made their fingers tingle. For the fifteenth time, Puggy Workman examined his gunlock and tested the working of the magazine, while the officers loosened their swords. Fordyce showed them the first resting place in their advance, and cautioned them to keep their heads. The men nodded without speaking, and felt the ground with their feet as a runner does in a race before the start.

The firing grew slower, and the billows of smoke lay sluggishly over the plain. Suddenly the artillery ceased, turned, and like a flash of lightning began pouring gun after gun into B's front, as they lay in close order behind the hillock. B yelled and groaned and sprang to their feet with a howl of rage that rang loud above the popping of the small arms and the banging of the cannon. The dead men rolled to one side, to avoid being trampled upon, and the gaping ranks closed up and charged up the hill, laughing in the very teeth of G's steady, rapid volleys and the raking cross-fire from the battery. E company, lying in reserve with fifty men, none gone, swept out to meet them. In another half minute, B would have been literally blown to pieces, but almost as E sprang from their hilltop, Company C, which had crept up unnoticed in the confusion, burst like a hailstorm in the fog on the reserves' left flank. Not knowing whence this sudden onslaught came, they pressed backward fearfully. Crash after crash of well-trained volleys poured from less than twenty feet into their surprised, serried ranks. Men cursed and howled and groaned and groped their way through smoke so thick that their course two yards ahead could scarcely be seen. Guns, useless, were thrown away, and the two front ranks grappled hand to hand and, swerving, gasped and choked while Company B, relieved, formed again and charged onward, their men, who should have been falling like wheat before the scythe, stubbornly refusing to die as ordered.

Meanwhile Fordyce with his six men came at a dog trot to their first grassy hummock and, stopping an instant, fired a few times at Company F, grinned happily, and raced on. No one seemed to pay much attention to them. Even F, their natural enemies, were using their might to aid in stemming the current of B's charge, and did not seem to see them. Not until they had arisen and had almost reached another spot of vantage ground, did any one in all that crowd on the hill seem to know them. Then suddenly Newton, standing with a knot of his classmates, gave a yell, and a moment later the crowd caught sight of them and, led by Newton, cheered with a mighty "Cornell, I yell, yell, yell, Cornell! D! D! D!"

The men heard it and chuckled, and Blake raised the colors from their leathern socket and waved them. Then the six dropped panting to the ground, and commenced again on F. Between the volleys, Puggy spoke, "I wonder what the matter is?"

"Give 'em time," said Tommy. "They

have n't waked yet. In a few minutes there will be worse yells than a T. N. E. swing."

"I feel like the 'Drums of the Fore and Aft,'" grunted Blake, waving his flag furiously as the two rifles cracked at once.

"Look, fellows," said Fordyce, pointing through a rift in the drifting smoke clouds, "G has struck her colors — she's surrendered, and to B, too."

"Look at Barker's gang, scrapping with E!" cried Blake, delightedly, the next minute. "Gosh! see Darwin hit that dago."

"H has already gone under," said Bug. "That leaves E yet, and the artillery. E will give up in a minute or two, and the others are likely to run at any moment now — unless all our plans are wrong. Their end approaches the second they begin to move around that clump of bushes. When we get by that pile of stones over there, and they see us, they will have to change position slightly to get a line on us. When that artillery shifts, some one is sure to hit one of those boxes, and they must be fairly alive by this time. You 'll see. Let 's go on, Jack."

" I 'm due to die by this next bush," said Puggy, mournfully, as they ran on over the rough ground. " I 've half a mind not to. If I do, I 'll lose all the fun."

" You die where you 're told to, Puggy," said Allerton, sternly. " You fellows have been in enough deviltry already. It will look a great deal better, and you will stand better chances of getting out without a bust, if you do as you 're told now."

" Wait and die with me," suggested Tommy. " Johnson is going to be there with pipes and water, and we 'll watch the victory. No one will notice. It 's just beyond this next tree here in the shade. Yeaaa! Johnson! See him?" Johnson waved his hand.

" All right," said Puggy. " I suppose that 's all right, is n't it, Allerton? Might as well?" Allerton nodded.

" Give Blake your gun before you go," said Fordyce, looking around. " *Some one 's* got to keep up the firing, you know. Allerton, you take the colors." Puggy and Tommy dropped dead with a sigh, and crawled over to Johnson and the water. Blake, whose heart had been yearning for a gun ever since the advance commenced, began loading and firing with amazing rapidity.

"There goes E," cried Bug to Fordyce; "I told you. *Now! Come on!*"

"Hold on!" ordered Fordyce, "who is commanding here? Steady. Wait until E gets out of the way, and then around to the right, so they will be forced to move to reach us. Yell as you run. Fire as often as you can, Blake, and, the rest of you, use both your revolvers. We've got to make them see us soon. Wait! Easy there, Blake — wait till — *now* — don't go too fast — give them time! *Charge!*"

With a whoop of savage anticipation, the four men swept over the rising land and, turning, ran slightly to the east. Fordyce led, his sword in one hand and a fiercely snapping Colt in the other. Allerton and Bug, with the flag and one revolver, were close seconds. Blake, having the heaviest load, brought up the rear, and, loading in a jolty, disjointed sort of way, poured shot after shot into the middle of Fordyce's back, and tore the air with blood-curdling cries. The crowd on the bank doubled up with laughter as the strange cavalcade came near. Even the staid old professors who had brought their wives smiled intellectually. Some of the blacksmith instructors went wild with joy, and a civil engineer became so excited that he clapped one of the assistants in chemistry on the shoulder, and swore hurriedly in Spanish. The sight was certainly most absurd, and Lieutenant Brainard, U. S. A., stood aghast. Four men with lolling tongues charging a battery and fifty was something quite unprecedented. Those next him heard him say things under his breath that he never would have said, had he remembered they were there. In a dazed way, he searched his memory for any mention of the regulations applicable in such a case, and for the first time his faith in himself wavered. This was good.

The next instant F caught sight of them, and Sawyer and the captain of the artillery gave a few quick orders. The men turned and, followed by the battery, raced across the hill, through the bushes, that they might form to charge when the time should come. As they hurried, some fell over square boxes that for some reason were hidden in the bushes. The two cannons in their race upset five, and the captain of the artillery, pausing a moment out of mere curiosity, was seen to rise quickly from his stooping position of investigation, and beat the air madly with his sabre, and, for some unaccountable reason, to turn back in the other direction. The men of F were loading with a viciousness that boded ill to the chuckling four in the hollow between the hills. Sawyer went from man to man, muttering, " Remember those uniforms, men," and each man scowled angrily and gripped his gun, while waiting for the word.

The charging four had slackened their pace

178

somewhat. Fordyce had seen the preparations for the charge, and, not wishing to be surrounded by a company so vastly his superior in numbers, was holding back.

The artillery began to load. F was waiting also. The watchers of D Company on the hillside began to hold their breaths.

"Heavens!" said Newton, nervously, "I wish they 'd get to work. I 've been five minutes ahead of a fit ever since they came across the hill."

Suddenly one man in Company F was seen to drop his gun and wave his arms wildly. Another followed with a yell of pain. Then one took off his hat and began to brandish it up and down, in a manner totally inexplicable to the spectators. The others followed quickly, and the contagion spread to the artillery. Its captain, far away in safety on the hillside, with the crowd, chuckled wickedly as he saw it. Then there followed a ludicrous sight. Man after man threw his gun down and, dancing madly up and down, struck viciously around

179

him, now with his helmet, now with his hands. Yells of pain, real pain this time, went up from over fifty voices. Men ran blindly for a few feet and, turning, struck madly at nothing. One man lay down on the ground and threw his coat over his head and hands. A moment later he fled, howling and limping. A peculiar buzzing sound filled his ears, and in half a second more the cry of "Bees! Bees! Run!" reached the four men of D Company, who were by this time rolling and gasping on the grass.

Panic-stricken F and the artillery, led by the doughty Sawyer, fled down the hill, followed by a cloud of bees that made the very air black. There were big bees and little bees and old bees and young bees, all flying, fighting, sting-ing mad, and after the blood of Company F, who had so presumptuously dared to disturb their rest. In vain F dodged and turned. In vain they beat the air. For every bee they crushed to earth a dozen rose again. Every ally that Blake and his companions had so gingerly and diplomatically brought from the university farm was doing its full duty. The retreat, which never had shown the slightest indication of being more dignified than a flight, now became a wild, disgraceful, stumbling run. Some fled east, some west, and some north, and the bees, with infinite cunning, separated into three divisions and followed, until they reached shelter.

Then the four heroes jogged leisurely to the hill and, capturing the enemy's standard, placed their own floating above the battery. The band, corralled by Puggy and Tommy, who had firmly refused to remain longer dead, marched up, bravely playing, " See the Conquering Hero Comes ! " and as the rest of the company who had cut joined the uniformed forces, a cheer went up from all the upper-classes that made the heavens tremble and the sun wince. Fordyce, Allerton, Bug, and Blake were thrown up shoulder high and by a dozen hands. Looking down on the sea of faces, each made a speech. Then the crowd joined hands and danced around them singing, —

" Fifty to four, fifty to four,
Company F is very sore."

This was Tommy Easton's composition, and he proudly led the chorus of voices.

On the hill, near-sighted professors smiled with satisfaction, and with their heads together nodded grave approval. Never before had a panic and retreat been so well acted they said. The professor of military science should certainly be congratulated. Hearing their enthusiastic descriptions and praise, the President of the University, who had strolled down from his house just after the flight was over, walked up to the professor of military science and complimented him in a pleasant way on the progress the troops seemed to have made. Lieutenant Wolsey R. Brainard, U. S. A., Commandant of the Cornell University Cadet Corps, did not reply, but showed his teeth. Then he started angrily across the field to D Company; then he turned back and gnawed his moustache.

It is said that there is now no man more bound by college traditions and precedents.

ONE WHO DIDN'T

183

ONE WHO DIDN'T

WILBUR lay flat on his back on the window-seat. A sophomore was pounding rag-time from the tortured piano at his head. Fifty feet away on the grass outside a freshman and a sub were laughing and tossing a baseball carelessly. Two juniors on the divan were talking earnestly and in low tones about the prospects for the next year. In the middle of the floor, Puggy Workman was dancing a right-footed clog, while Torresdale looked on with grave amusement.

From the piazza of a nearby fraternity house came the sounds of girlish voices, mingling with the music of mandolins and guitars. Strolling up and down the campus sidewalk, seniors in gowned solemnity knocked elbows with each other.

Wilbur lay flat on his back on the window-seat. He did not hear the cries of the fresh-man; he did not even notice the din of the piano.

Ordinarily, he took the keenest interest in the living panorama passing up and down the hill before his eyes. To-day, he did not see it; to-day, his thoughts were all he had, for yesterday his class had been graduated — and he had not been with them.

The trouble had been that during his college course his ambition had winged too high, and the duties pertaining to the leadership of the Glee Club, the presidency of the Masque, and the managership of the baseball team, piling one after another upon him, had been proved to be more than one man ought to carry. To be sure, he had intended to give the Masque entirely up to the business manager; but somehow or other the business manager had not been as enthusiastic in some ways as he should have been, and he had been afraid that something would go wrong. It had not been absolutely necessary for him to go on that last trip with the baseball team, and Fordyce could have attended to everything just as well, after the way had been made smooth for him; but in some way he felt that he *must* go, just to make things sure. It was not his nature to trust things to his assistants. If he had charge of anything, he always wanted to do the work himself; and so he had cut lecture after lecture, and had neglected to make up a term of junior drawing, all of which had resulted in the omission of his name from the lists of graduating students posted in front of the registrar's office. It was of no use to protest.

His bed was made. Simply because he had worked for the good of the university, and worked hard that his Alma Mater should be known, as well by her success in athletics, dramatics, and music, as by the standard of her examinations, was no reason why the university should be lenient and allow him his sheepskin. If such a thing were so, there would be great confusion. This was what A Certain Mighty

Personage, who rubbed his chin complacently, had said to Johnson. Therefore it must be so.

So Wilbur lay flat on his back on the window-seat, and in the midst of all the noise and action around him, he was as much alone as if he had been at the bottom of Fall Creek Gorge. Marching in a funereal cavalcade, his memories passed through his mind. He remembered vividly the day he saw his name was absent from the roll of his class, and he remembered how he had thought that with a little study and one or two petitions he should still get through all right. He had not thought of that miserable junior drawing then, and he had still his old confidence in himself. He recalled his father's proud but anxious shake of his head when he had told him, in his Christmas vacation, that he had been elected president of The Masque. His father had been afraid that too many outside honors would imperil his graduation; but he had laughed his fears to scorn — then. Now it was his father's turn to laugh, if he had wished, but he did not. He merely wrote that he was sorry, and that he and the rest of the family were very much disappointed. That was all; but Wilbur knew the look that had come into his father's eyes, as well as if he had seen it, and he knew too that although nothing more would ever be said on the subject, his failure would never be forgotten.

This was bad enough, but the worst of it all was, that it was not as if he had the excuse of thoughtless procrastination. It was not as if he had only been foolish, like so many of his classmates. He had, open-eyed and deliberately, chosen his path, and that way danger lay. He had pounded on with all his confidence and assurance unshaken, sure that he could accomplish what he had undertaken, and now that he had failed, the cup was doubly bitter because of the blow to his pride.

Like many men, he had found a grim pleasure in self-chastisement. He had donned the cap and gown with the rest, even after he knew his fate. The swishing skirt reminded him constantly that he had no right to wear it, and

with every step seemed to be saying, Failure!
Failure! Failure! in remorseless whispers. He
did not mind this, he said to himself bitterly.
He deserved it, and. it was but right that his
punishment should be severe. Failure was the
one thing that was hardest of all for him to for-
give in others, and now that his time had come
he should not flinch.

With religious flagellation he had continually
sought those associations that he deemed would
be most painful. He had tramped up the hill to
vote for his class officers; and when the class
wanted to run him for orator, he explained that
he was sorry, but he had neglected his work, and
would not be graduated that year. This had
hurt terribly; but it was some satisfaction to
remember that the class had elected him over
such a disgrace, and for a while the blackness of
his cloud had seemed touched with silver.

In the days following the discovery of his
failure, he had suffered and become hardened to
many things. After a few weeks, when strolling
down the hill, with an arm on a classmate's

shoulder, it was not hard to say casually, "Going to get through all right?" and to reply with well-assumed unconcern to the answer and question that invariably followed, "No, I am afraid not. Beastly junior drawing." The pipe had often been a great help, for it could be chewed and wobbled around in his mouth so that the strange quality in his voice could not be detected. Now he did not need even the pipe. The fellows would usually say, "By Jove, old man, that's hard luck. I'm sorry," and then would mention it to two or three others, and forget about it. This was natural enough, and Wilbur knew it and understood. Many men would have argued that because their classmates had so easily forgotten, they were no longer their friends. This is foolish and selfish, and Wilbur was neither.

But all this was over now, and Wilbur lay among the cushions staring drearily into the nothingness of the future and the happiness of the past. They seemed to dance before him hand in hand, while the sophomore beat the piano and Puggy danced a right-footed clog. He remembered with what a choking, blinding sensation he had stood at the bay-window and watched the fellows marching together to the armory to their graduation. He remembered how, as the dear old familiar faces passed, his heartstrings tugged and pulled with a yearning he had never known before. Then, when all had passed through the armory door, and stood with their heads bowed in the solemn reverence of the hour and the prayer, he remembered how he had fled to his room and, his spirit broken at last, had buried his face in the pillows and cried like a child. He need not have been ashamed of it, but his face flushed even now at the memory. Then he remembered how he had stolen, while the President was speaking, to an old bush on the campus, near where his class would march and smoke their pipe and sing their songs and plant their ivy. He had sat there with a heart-sickness that made him far too miserable to care who saw or knew him.

He remembered just how that long black-robed line of figures had looked, as they came marching up the campus. There was Johnson; there was Torresdale. There were Blake and Cuthbert and Farnsworth and Thompson, the captain of the baseball team, with whom he had slept and eaten and lived and breathed so long that term. There was Josh Groswild walking with Lyndhurst; there was the Co-ed *Era* editor; there was Katzenkönig, who had come from Heidelberg, — he had counted them all mechanically.

A dozen times he had risen to go away somewhere, and lie face downwards and pull up great tufts of grass, and a dozen times he had fallen back again by the bush. He could not go, yet he did not want to stay, and he was sure his heart was breaking. He remembered that a long time ago, when his brother had died, he had felt something the same way. He had wondered why they all looked so grave, and there had been one man in whose eyes he had actually seen tears. This was rather foolish, he thought. What had he to mourn over?

13   193

They were all there, — all his friends, all his
four years' companions, all *his class :* his class,
with whom he had entered, risen, rushed, quar-
relled, loved, and hated, all together, — together, since the days when, as boyish freshmen,
each man had played at mumblety-peg with
his neighbor, while waiting for his turn to
register; together, since the times when, as
mighty sophomores, they had victoriously
rushed the timid freshmen — and won the flag,
down by Percy Field; together, through the
privileges of the first year of upper-classman-
ship; and now finally, when the whirling, rushing, remorseless stream of time had borne them
all too quickly through the years of college life,
they were again together. Hand in hand,
shoulder to shoulder, heart to heart, they were
to step from the green meadows of their Alma
Mater over the stile, and into the rough, uneven
roads of life, and he — could not be with them.

He remembered just how they had sat in the
circle, and how the pipe had gone around and
around, and how one co-ed had choked and

coughed at the taste of smoke. He had giggled hysterically, he remembered, and had wondered for a flash why none of them had laughed. Then he had become savagely indignant at the sisters and mothers and fathers looking on because they had smiled.

Then how well he remembered Gordon's face as the class rose in a body, and he led them in Alma Mater. It was the face of an angel glorified. How the old thrill ran through him, again and again, as the air rose and fell and the line marched slowly down the campus, two abreast; and how his whole heart and soul had cried to be with them. The agony of that minute had been supreme, and with that wish there came again the rending sorrow of knowing he had no right in their ranks, of knowing that his class had gone and he was left.

It was strange, he thought, that he had not known until now how much he cared about them all. He had not believed that it would be so hard to have them go. Maybe in a few months he would get over it. But still — he had failed

— he was disgraced, he thought, and that, though time could make it but a memory, could never be effaced. Things would never be the same. His father would never have the same confidence in him. There would be another line of sorrow in his mother's face. People at home would say among themselves, " I hear young Wilbur did n't pass up there at Cornell," and would nod their heads gravely and raise their eyebrows, just as they had done when his father's clerk had embezzled some of his money, and the newspapers took it up. He could see their faces now.

The sophomore, who really played well when he wished, had drifted from rag-time to Sousa, and from Sousa, with what was seemingly a swift boyish change of mood, to Schumann's Nachtstück. The rest had gone to dinner, and had yelled to Wilbur to come on. Wilbur had replied, in his natural voice, telling them to go ahead, and he would be down directly. They had gone, and now Wilbur heard the rattling of knives and forks, and the clatter of many voices

in the dining-room below. They did not understand, he thought. Why should they? Men
to-day did not mingle with men whose heads
were bowed and whose flapping sackcloth
tempted every wind. One's face was no longer
a barometer of one's feelings. Besides — those
others had not failed. They had never even
tasted such bitterness as had fallen to him.

When one feels as Wilbur did, one is likely to
overestimate his own suffering and underesti-
mate the misfortunes of his friends. Disappoint-
ment, with all its retinue of grief and shame, is
usually selfish and self-centred, and the person
across whose drawbridge the host once rides,
often unwittingly drops the portcullis behind
them.

This is bad, and the sophomore who did not
understand, knew it. He had been " busted " in
his freshman year, and had felt the same way.
So he played Schumann's Nachtstück. He played
it very, very softly at first, so that when Wilbur
closed his eyes, the music seemed to be made by
a faint breath of wind far off among the stars.

Somehow the running fulness of the chords was filled with a special meaning for him to-day. There was a passionate note of melancholy appeal somewhere there that accorded well with his sorrow, and with an inexplicable paradox there stole into his heart a deep, full sense of comfort that drove away all the despair and sorrow. He felt like stretching his arms out to something. His heart felt less hopeless, and as there came a change in the music, and the bass joined with the treble in a brief song of triumph, he forgot entirely, for the moment, all his failure. Then as the last few solemn notes. fell slowly, one after another, with a kind of warning mournfulness, he remembered once more, and the wave of remorse and sorrow swept rushing back again.

Yet there was a difference, — a very subtle difference, but one that changed things wonderfully, and left him pondering. All the sorrow and all the yearning for his class still held his heart, but where before the future had seemed blank, and where the past had seemed foolish, there was now hope and a lesson. He wondered vaguely why this was. But a moment before there had been nothing left in all the world to live for. Now there seemed to be a great deal in life still left to him. He remembered now that only yesterday one of the fellows had put his arm over his shoulder and said, "Billy, old man, it 's mighty hard luck for you, — your not graduating; but I 'm awfully glad you 're going to be back next year. We need you." It made him feel rather good and warm inside to think about it. He recalled other little incidents which, when they occurred had not made much impression upon him, but which he now understood. For instance, when Puggy Workman had come to him, his round, good-natured face all wreathed in smiles, and said, " I hear you 're going to be with us next year. Good work." It had n't seemed at all good work then, but now — well, perhaps it was not so bad. Still, you know, it was his class, and he had n't — and it was hard not to be able to march and sing the songs. The other class was all right, but they were n't *his* class. There weren't any Johnsons or Fultons or Blakes among the juniors. If he had only studied harder, he might have — what was that tune the sophomore was playing? — it was certainly very beautiful and comforting. It was a little sleepy too. Perhaps if he — should see the Dean he might let him — how far away that music seemed. He didn't know the sophomore could play so well. Still the Dean had told him before then that there could be no leniency. He could easily — what *was* that tune? He had heard it somewhere before. Somewhere — a good many years ago, wasn't it? Or was it — maybe it was nearly time to go down to dinner now. He would just — it had been his fault; all his fault — still, it was his class — his very own — and they couldn't — what an ugly word failure was. Why did they always spell it in such large capitals? He had never noticed it up there beside the chandelier before. It was certainly queer. How very sleepy that music was . . . if he — it was his class — and he had not . . . but still . . .

The sophomore let his fingers fall with a sigh of relief. He was tired. It is rather tiring for any one to play the same thing over and over without stopping once, and it is especially so when one is watching some one else out of the corner of one's eyes.

.   .   .   .

Wilbur lay flat on his back on the window-seat, and the sophomore rose with an unconscious sigh and smiled inscrutably as he looked down on his quiet slumbers.

"I thought it would," he said. "It generally does." And then he bent down and shook him gently. "Hi, there, old man, dinner!" he said loudly.

And only the Nachtstück knew exactly what he meant.

ONE WHO DID

ONE WHO DID

THE three-car train backed, puffing and panting, up the steep grade of the second switch. Fordyce, with a curious straining in his throat, and a misty damp feeling in his eyes, stood on the rear platform of the last car looking out across the valley.

High on the hills the buildings of the University stood clearly outlined against the summer sky. The afternoon sunlight fell across them all, — Morrill, White, McGraw, the Physical Lab., the Chemical Lab., and all the rest, — making the roofs of the newer buildings glisten and shine. North of the others, the dumpy little observatory stood forlornly alone, its one small telescope looking out of its curved roof, round-eyed and disconsolate. Further down the hill, the top of the flag pole in front of the gymnasium and the gables of two fraternity houses broke the line of tree-tops, and across the bridge the gray, windowed walls of the old Cascadilla dormitory marked the entrance to the campus. The leaves in the trees hung quietly, mourning the death of the afternoon breeze, and from the shops to the bridge there was hardly a sign of life. Even the old town of Ithaca itself, clinging to the hillside, and stretching over the lowlands, seemed still and lifeless. Beyond Renwick, the lake lay without a ripple, in its nest of forests, reflecting every cloud or bird which sailed across the June sky.

Fordyce was going home.

The spring term was ended, and the university had stopped to breathe. This year three hundred and four men had been graduated. Men from the North, the South, the East, the West, men·from England, men from Scotland, men from Japan, men from Spain, men from the Hawaiian Islands, men from almost everywhere, who had earnestly, flippantly, merrily, stolidly, lived and studied together for four whole years, were now scouring the country in search of positions, or packing their flannels and outing clothes for one last long vacation.

Senior week had been gayer than usual. There had been more pretty girls, dances, boat rides, and drives than ever before, and the Senior Ball Committee had made their part of the week so far outshine the Senior Balls of the past that they were scarcely remembered.

Fordyce looked back over it, and told himself that he had enjoyed it all most gloriously. Then he looked further back. It was this that caused that mistiness and the queer feeling in his throat.

It is hard for a man to leave his college and all its associations forever. The thread of its life is very slender, and, once broken, all but impossible to tie. If one is absent but a year, he finds on his return that half his friends are gone and their places filled with newer men with whom he has nothing in common and whom he does not even know. He loses track of things, and when his remaining friends gather in his room, use his tobacco, tear leaves out of his books for spills, and talk over the things that have happened, he is hopelessly at sea, and has to ask who Dick is, or Tom who? or in what class is Harry? It takes a long time to get back the old feeling of oneness; and even when new friends are made, and fresh associations formed (which if one had not had the others would be just as satisfying), there is always the feeling that those who are new never knew those whom you knew, and thus one note is lost from the fulness of the chord.

Fordyce thought of all this, for his father had offered him two more years in the Law School. He knew that he had finished the pleasantest chapters of his twenty-two years. He knew that his work, so far from being done, was but in its beginning, and he appreciated the enormous possibilities which the broader field brought to him. He felt guilty as he looked back across those hills, and the old love welled up into his heart, for he was not at all sure that he cared about enormous possibilities, or a chance to show what was in him. And there was the Law School!

He saw its stone sides as the train puffed on. He had no intention of ever practising law, but it would be very pleasant to spend two more years there. Then too a legal education was never wasted, and, maybe, if he knew a little law, business would open up better.

He stood with one foot on the railing, and behind him his hands grasped the platform handles. The little driblets of smoke floated from his pipe to the edge of the rushing wind at the car side, and one after another were caught and blown to pieces. Inside, the car was crowded with students and their guests of the week going home. They were all singing, and one fellow was sitting on the back of a seat playing banjo accompaniments. Several chaperons sat in one corner. They smiled indulgently at his boisterousness. They had been smiling indulgently at everything for so long that week that the smile had almost become a habit, and would fly to their faces mechanically,

even if one only said, "Scat!" or scratched a
match somewhere near them.

But Fordyce was not in the humor for this
gayety, — at least not now, he said to himself.
He wanted to stand on the rear platform and
think, until the college should be far out of
sight. Moreover, he did not exactly see how
the seniors who were never coming back could
bear to laugh and sing and joke in such a heart-
less way. There was certainly nothing to laugh
at. He had not yet learned that this was what
many people do when they do not wish to think
about things.

How much had happened since first, as a lowly
freshman, he had trudged up and down that hill
to recitations! There was a car crawling up
State Street now! When he first came a car line
was not even thought of, and the crew used to run
up and down the steepest parts of Buffalo Street
to get their wind, and bring the calves of their
legs into proper shape. There had been a little
horse-car running from the hotel to the station,
but that was all. How many, many times he

and his chum Burleigh had tumbled out of bed
in that old red house over there on Stewart
Avenue, and raced all the way up the hill as
fast as their legs could carry them, to make an
eight o'clock in White or Morrill Hall. Burleigh was a good fellow, he thought, and it
was a pity that his father had died just as he
was commencing his second year. They had
been pretty much together, and both had been
pledged to the same fraternity when Burleigh
left. He had not joined, but Fordyce had, and
how well he remembered it all! How embarrassed he had felt when he was being rushed,
and how queer it had been to see an upper-classman offer him his seat, or get him a match for
his pipe! What a nice crowd of fellows they
were, and how he had trembled and felt a sort of
numbness all over when Collingwood, a senior
then, and an object of terrible awe, had put his
hand on his shoulder, and said solemnly, " Jack,
I should like to speak to you for a few moments.
Will you come up to my room ? " He laughed
at himself when it was over; but he had always

known how others who were being rushed felt, and he had consequently treated them very kindly.

Then there had been the time that he and Blake had been so nearly expelled for climbing up the inside of the Sibley chimney, while the fires were burning, and fastening a tin flag, with their class numerals painted thereon, to the very topmost outside brick. If there had not been a few young professors on the faculty who admired the daring of the feat, they would have received much more than the solemn reprimand and warning as they stood tremblingly before them. That had been the beginning of the firm friendship between Blake and himself.

He wondered where all the fellows would be a year from now; scattered to the four corners of the earth, he supposed. He did not even know where he should be. At all events, it was all over now. There would be no more sitting around Zinckes and singing the old songs on winter evenings. There would be no more Savage Club gatherings and good times together. The Sibley Dinner Pail Brigade was disorganized, and the pails were lying abandoned in the vacant rooms. In the fall, freshmen would come and take the rooms and pails. He wondered who would have his. He had never known who had used it before him; but he had become quite attached to it, and he hoped that it would not fall into unappreciative hands.

But it was not any one thing that he so regretted leaving, he thought; it was not the baseball, the football, or the tennis, even if he *had* held the intercollegiate championship in the latter; nor was it the free and easy life one could lead with a lot of fellows; it was not the Masque, or the Glee Club, or the Savage Club, or any other one of the ways in which he had enjoyed himself, — it was the knowledge that he was turning his back on all these things. In themselves, they were not of any great importance, but the secret was his love for their associations. For instance, there was that long bench in White 10, where Professor Black held his lectures on French Literature. There was nothing to attract one to it, but Fordyce had sat there every Monday, Wednesday, and Friday at nine for two college years, and he knew every pencil-mark or knife scratch around the seat. He knew every crack in the floor and mark on the walls of the room. He knew just when he would be called upon, and he knew the exact location of the hairpin which was always on the point of dropping from the back hair of the co-ed on the front seat. Then, too, he had sat next to Griggs, the 'varsity stroke, and a very nice chap. He remembered that Griggs used to pinch the man in front of him, and then say, "Ouch! Quit that!" very audibly; and when Professor Black would look very reprovingly at the man in front, and request the class to keep better order, Griggs would look in an injured way at him, and nod his head as if to say, "That's right! Good! A man really can't attend to his lesson if that goes on, you know," and then would go into gales of laughter as soon as the professor turned away.

Now a man cannot go in and out the same

buildings, up and down the same stairways, and to and fro on the same road for four years with a crowd of his friends, doing as they do, sharing their lot, and sitting by their sides, without growing to love the buildings, the stairways, and the road. He may not know he loves them until after he leaves them. While he is tramping in and out, and up and down, he may consider that he is undergoing a terrible grind, and he may believe he hates the sight of the steps and the recitation-rooms; but the instant he leaves them forever, he is conscious of all their latent charms. There have been many men who in the midst of the din and turmoil of business-life have become suddenly conscious of an inexplicable yearning for the steps of old White Hall; and Fordyce, pulling at his empty pipe, was not the first who had felt that species of homesickness.

It certainly seemed longer ago than yesterday that he and Blake had strolled over the campus, taking their last farewell of all their old haunts. It must have been longer ago than that when

215

they stood in the centre of the old athletic field, and looked around in silence at all their old stone friends. Then they had walked back of the Fiske-McGraw, and, lying on the grass, had watched the sun slowly sinking beyond the lake. He remembered that they had not spoken for a long time. There had been little need of speech, for both were watching with a sad intensity as the sun crept slowly nearer the crimson horizon. They felt as though dusk had overtaken them at the foot of the lane, and that to-morrow the sun would rise upon paths of which they knew nothing, on paths which led far away from the old buildings and the campus and each other, and sometimes that there might be paths on which the sun did not shine. And yet it was not the future itself, but the past which was so soon to be that caused their silence. It was the knowledge that to-morrow the new life began and the old life ended — and the old life was inexpressibly dear.

Then he remembered how at last the sun had set, and Blake had suddenly buried his face in his hands, and said, in an odd sort of voice, "Jack, it's all over!" He said nothing in reply, but slipped an arm around his neck, and they had sat for some time looking out across the hills, while the shadows faded from the waters of the lake, and the skies melted slowly from red to gold. Finally, he rose and said, "Come on, old man," to Blake, and Blake had stumbled to his feet, pushed back his hair, and set his hat firmly on his head. They walked down the campus, talking of other things, but, as they reached Sage, both had turned and looked back for a moment.

Now, after all that, here Blake was laughing and singing with the girls and fellows inside the car, as if he had forgotten that there ever was a last night. How people could laugh when they were leaving college forever, he did not understand!

Then he thought of the Law School once more. Really, he thought, a legal education was just the thing to top off with. After that and his four years' course in M. E., he would be ready for almost anything; he would have a fully rounded education. He did not believe in onesidedness, and he thought it possible that now, with only one degree, he — and he had always heard that law was extremely pleasant work. Moreover, Wilbur was coming back, and he and Wilbur could room together, and — and he would not have to leave it all just yet. That was the main argument, he thought: he would not have to leave it all just yet. There were so many things he had not done and would now like to do. He would like to finish that Masque play. He would like to run for Commodore of the crew, and go to Poughkeepsie when they rowed Yale the next year. He would like to have a try at the baseball managership, too, and he would like to be again with the Glee Club.

Then the words of his mother's last letter, written just after he had passed his last examination, flashed into his mind. "Chicago is so far away," she had written, "that your father and I do not feel as if we could afford to come

on to your graduation. It has been a great dis-
appointment to us both; but we are happy in the
hope of soon seeing you again, and having you
with us for all time. Your father counts greatly
upon your help in his business, as, ever since
the store burned, he has not been as well, and
I know that he looks forward to your coming."

Fordyce flushed with shame.

Here he was thinking of going back for
two more years! It was not right. It could
not be right that he should be enjoying himself, even if he was studying, while his father
needed him. In most instances a law course
might be a very good thing; but — moreover, he
would be spending more money, and though no
one at home had ever said anything about his
expenses, he knew how hard it had been to keep
him at college.

. . . .

Fordyce leaned over and knocked the ashes
out of his pipe. He certainly would not take
those extra two years. He had been a fool, he
thought, for even thinking about them. He

would make up his mind now, once and for all,
to put such thoughts away. More than that,
he was glad — he was very glad that he was
not going back. If he couldn't go, he might
just as well make up his mind to it, he thought,
and there was no use in feeling blue about it
anyway. So he was glad, he was sure of it.

Still — What a lucky fellow Wilbur was!
He had failed to be sure, but he didn't seem
to mind it a bit, and laughed and joked about
his being there next year quite as if it were the
thing to be "busted." He was fortunate not
to have very deep feelings, he thought. Yes,
he should certainly like to go back with
Wilbur; but it was not best. Anyway, after
one has had four years of college, it is time for
him to do something. At the same time —
But, pshaw! He had decided that he was glad.
How extremely annoying it was to forget such
a thing! There was no real need of his remind-
ing himself of it, — at least there should not
be. It was very simple. He was glad. What
more? He would go into the car and sing and

laugh with Blake, and get Torresdale angry by talking nonsense with that little Miss What's-her-name from Buffalo. It was fun to get Torresdale angry. He would do that.

Fordyce looked up. He saw that the train had passed Caroline five minutes before, and that he had not noticed. The University was far behind, out of sight beyond the hills.

The mistiness in his eyes, and the curious straining in his throat, came back again with a sudden rush. He felt like screaming, " I can't go! I *can't!* I CAN'T!" but he waited quietly until the mistiness had gone away and his throat felt natural again. Then he walked into the car and stopped at the water-cooler. He looked around him. The fellow was still playing the banjo, and Fordyce, tiptoeing softly behind him, gave a slight sudden jerk, and he fell, — a mass of tangled legs and arms and banjo, while the crowd shrieked wildly with joy, and the chaperons smiled indulgently. In a moment he emerged between two seats, his face one huge grin.

Fordyce sat down by the girl from Buffalo.

" I am very glad," he said.

The girl turned wonderingly.

" Why — why — thank you," she answered.

But Fordyce only smiled.

THE ELDER MISS ARCHLEN

THE ELDER MISS ARCHLEN

H E was a good freshman. One of the kind that buy the upper-classmen cigarettes, and go to the door when the bell first rings, instead of waiting an hour or so to see if any one else is going. He was all around the best freshman we had that year. The others — well, you know — did n't believe in upper-class discipline and made sarcastic remarks when seniors made mistakes. The rest were of that class.

The good Freshman made one mistake, though. It was in this way.

One evening, rather early, several of us were sitting around the upper-classmen's table at Pat's. We had sung ourselves out and Blake was not there to tell us any new stories, so we fell to smoking silently. Once or twice Rogers hit the bottom of his beer-glass on the table,

15   225

and a little while afterward we all turned them upside down and hit the tops. Morley gloomily studied the different names cut in the soft pine table. Cuthbert, sprawling with his coat wide open, was idly shying crackers at "Puggy" Workman's mouth. Fordyce was scratching all the matches to obtain charcoal wherewith to ink in his newly-cut name; and the rest of us, except the Freshman, to whom we had accorded our gracious permission to sit with us that evening, were staring wearily at the revolving fans above us, and wondering how they could bear to move so fast on such a scorching day. Over in the corner, Marnit sat, white-aproned and perspiring, only rising now and then when one of us hit the table.

Suddenly the Freshman broke the silence with, "Say, fellows, can I have a girl on for Senior Week?"

We all withdrew our gaze from the ceiling, and Morley paused with his knife poised, just as he was about to cut a period after a P. G.'s neglected name.

"Certainly, why not?" said he.

The Freshman reddened. He was not used to so much attention, and murmured something unintelligible about, "Did n't know — freshman — girls —" and timidly took a sip of beer.

Morley looked at him wisely. "Is she a peach?" he said. I saw the Freshman's hand make just the slightest motion in the world toward his upper left-hand vest-pocket as he replied, "I 'll show you her picture — up at the house sometime. Yes, I think she is pretty."

"Of course," said Cuthbert, under his breath.

The Freshman caught the mumbled words and assumed a half-defiant air.

"When is she coming?" asked Puggy, in a crackery voice.

"I 'm going to ask her for the week — if that 's all right."

"Sure," said I.

"And," asked Johnson, from a smoke cloud, "what" — puff — "is her" — puff — "name?"

"Archlen, a Miss Edith Archlen," replied the Kid.

Morley woke suddenly, "Edith Archlen? Of Buffalo?"

"Yes," apprehensively.

"Well, I'll be — Edith Archlen! I knew her two years ago, — knew her well all one summer at Block Island. The Kid has sense, fellows. She's all right and can dance, too. There were mighty few college men down there that summer, and we — Oh, well!" Morley winked solemnly at the man on his right, and stared whimsically into his glass.

The Freshman caught the wink and reflected. Then the corners of his mouth tightened a little, and he looked earnestly at Morley.

"Well?" said the latter.

. "Nothing."

Morley looked at him curiously and rose.
. "Let's go to Renwick, fellows," he yawned. "It's cooler there, and there is a rather clever vaudeville in the pavilion. Come on."

We all considered the proposition favorably,

except the Freshman. He begged off on the plea of work, and we saw him disappear up the hill as we were waiting for our car.

When I came in that night I found him waiting for me. I roomed with him then. He wheeled in his chair to face me, and looked on in silence while I cast off enough of my garments to keep cool. Then when I had cocked my feet on the desk, and tucked a couple of cushions in my chair, he said solemnly, "Billy, it's Morley."

I looked around the room, and not knowing in the least what he was talking about, said, "No!" incredulously.

"Don't, Billy. I'm in earnest. I — you know — about Edith."

"Oh!" said I, understandingly, for he had relieved himself by long talks with me when the pressure had grown too great, and I knew what he thought of Miss Archlen.

"You mean Morley is the fellow who used to know her so well and whom she liked so much?"

"Yes, and I —"

"Don't know whether to ask her here or not?"

"Well, you see she will stay here with her mother, and Morley will be in the same house, and it would be rather — rather — would n't it?"

"She likes you, does n't she?" I asked.

The Freshman pretended a yawn of unconcern, and said, "I think so."

I was inexorable. "Don't you know so?"

"I — I think I do."

"Well," said I, "don't be a fool."

"I know," he said; "but Morley is so infernally good-looking and clever. If she liked him so much when he was younger and not so — so — you know, why won't she like him all the more now?"

"Girls' tastes change as they grow older," said I, with senioric wisdom.

"But they always like pretty things and candy, don't they?"

"Possibly," I admitted; "but does not your mirror show —"

"Oh, shut up, Billy!" said he, elegantly. "I'm in earnest, — terribly in earnest, if I am a freshman."

My pipe was bubbling as I thought hard for a few minutes. Rising, I knocked out the ashes. "Old man," I said, "are you really and truly in love with Miss Archlen?"

He made a brave attempt at a smile as he said, "If I am not, it's the most realistic fake I ever ran up against."

"And things look dismal?" I continued.

"Very!" he replied.

"Well," said I, "you go in and win. I'll help you all I know how, and between us I guess Morley won't cut much ice."

He grabbed my hand gratefully. "Will you?" he said. "I know you can help lots. You're so much brighter than the rest, and know exactly what to do in a case of push."

"Come to bed," said I, with affected sleepiness, "for I hate scenes. You do your best, and I'll see what I can do about Morley."

Just before he turned out the light he brought

out a square object from the breast-pocket of his pajamas, and held it up before me in silence.

"She's all right," said I.

"Good-night," he answered, stroking the brass knob on my bed tenderly. He knew that I understood.

I walked up the campus the next morning with Morley, and asked him if he was going to have any one up for the Senior.

"Not if the Kid has Miss Archlen," he replied. "I can entertain her, you know, while he is fixing up the box and all that. I think I can find enough for him to do, too. Queer, wasn't it, the way he acted last night about it? Oh, well — others have been just as far gone as he, and it won't hurt him to have a fall taken out of him."

"Oh, let him alone," said I, "you don't want her and he does."

"He thinks he does," said Morley, "that's all. So long," and he dropped off at Morrill.

My mind was made up. I should show my classmate no mercy. Morley was a mighty nice

chap, but possessed of a surpassing knowledge
of his own powers in every line. There was no
doubt that he was clever and good-looking, but
he occasionally let his desire to show his powers
run away with his judgment.

That evening at dinner an idea flashed into
my mind. After dinner I whistled to the Freshman. He came, looking pale and worried, to
where I sat in comfort watching the redness
of the sunset. "What do you want, Billy?"
said he.

"First, a cigarette," said I.

He handed it to me in silence.

"Well," I observed.

"Well," he repeated.

"Are n't you forgetting yourself?" said I.

"I beg your pardon, Billy," said he, and
handed me the wherewithal.

I lit up, puffed contentedly for a moment, and
told the Freshman to sit down. He sat.

"Kid," said I, "is Miss Archlen Miss Archlen or Miss Edith Archlen?"

"What the —" he began.

"Wait," I interrupted commandingly; "what I mean is, has she an older sister?"

"Yes, why?"

"How much older?" I asked.

"Two years, but —"

"How old is Ed — Miss Edith?"

"Twenty," he answered, with smouldering fire in his eye.

"Is her older sister any good?"

"She's very bright and pretty, dances like Crawford's sister, and is mighty good fun. She is not as pretty as Edith, though. You know Edith has that funny wavy brown hair like — like —"

"Prexy's horse blanket," I suggested.

The Freshman subsided.

"Now, see here," I went on, "does Morley know her?"

"No."

"Do you know her — well, I mean?"

"Yes."

"Do you think she would come down for the week with her sister if you asked her?"

"In a minute," he said; "but — "

"One moment," I had to remind him. "Now listen. That is my last Senior week, and I'm girlless. I was going to trot my younger sister around, but she's sailed for Europe, and that lets me out. From what you say, I imagine Miss Archlen is pretty smooth, and, anyway, if she dances like Polly Crawford, she can have me — for the week. I want you to write up there telling her all about me, enclosing my card, and asking her to come here for the house party as a guest of the society, on your invitation."

"But I'm going to take — " began the Freshman.

"I know you are," said I. "You are going to ask both and take one, — either one you want, — I'll take the other. Write up and tell her so. Write to-night. She will come if you explain things, won't she?"

"Oh, she'll *come* all right, all right," said he; "only what in the devil, Billy, has all this rot to do with Morley?"

I nearly fell off my chair with laughter. "Why, you idiot!" said I, when I could catch my breath, "everything. You do as I tell you. Write to Buffalo to-night. Put it strong. Both the girls must come or you are lost; they are your only salvation. *Both*, mind you — and Kid," I continued, in a ruminative way, "1 shall have to ask you to make out both the cards. I am getting rather old to hustle around after dances, you know. I suppose Morley will want several with Miss Edith Archlen. He'll come to you for them. Don't worry about looking him up. When he does come, he will ask to see Miss Archlen's card. Give it to him! Give him all he wants; but — but — Oh, you fool!" I roared, for the expression of imbecile happiness that was dawning on his face was more than mortal man could bear.

The idea of Morley, the elegant, all sufficient, omnipotent, overpowering Morley, being sold was too much. We pictured his serene self-satisfaction as he wrote his name in a dozen places over Miss Edith Archlen's elder sister's card. We saw vividly just how he felt when he found it out. We tasted the foaming tankards that he would buy when it was all over, and then we laughed again. Finally, when we had squeezed the subject mirthless for the present, we put our heads together.

"Billy," said the Freshman, "Morley must n't know you are going to take Miss Archlen."

"He won't," said I.

"And the thing must n't seem too easy," he continued.

"Your lookout," said I; "give me a match."

"Suppose he wants to take her to the Masque or Concert, or any of the other dances, or to the boat ride?"

"Same scheme," I replied. "His money is as good as mine any day."

"Billy, I don't know how to — I — you 're a — dog gone it all, Billy, have another cigarette?"

"Kid," said I, taking it, "if you don't get to work, that prelim. in Analytics is going to hit you right where a man finds it hard to shave," and I walked over to talk with Blake.

Things went right our way from the start. I put the fellows up to waking Morley's desire to monopolize the younger Miss Archlen by a judicious course of guying, until finally he went around with his handsome head in the air and a light of determination in his eyes. As soon as the Freshman started making out the dance cards, Morley swooped down upon him, and, by some very skilful manœuvring, managed to get twelve dances with the elder sister, and went away chuckling. A day later I arranged to have several of the fellows appear at once, and plead for the honor of Miss Archlen's company at the Concert, including the buying of tickets, roses, and carriage hire. Morley was there. After much competition and persuasion, the Freshman gave in to him. He was delighted, and insisted on paying me the sum of a dollar and a half, which he had owed me ever since he went broke at the last football game.

The Freshman was jubilant, and talked in his sleep. Toward the end of the week, Morley

stopped me in front of the Armory. "Billy,"
said he, "I have a favor to ask of you."

"Go ahead," said I.

"It's this way," said he. "I want to take
Miss Archlen to the boat ride."

"Of course," said I.

"Eh?" said he.

"You can," said I.

"Wha-at?" said he.

"You were saying —" I observed.

Morley stared.

"I want to take Miss Archlen to the boat
ride," he said. "If you have gone crazy or —"

"I beg your pardon, Morley," said I. "I was
not thinking of Senior week just then."

"I want to take Miss Archlen to the boat
ride," he repeated.

"Well, why don't you?" I asked.

"You see, that's just it," he answered. "I
have bullied the Kid out of twelve dances for
the Senior, and wheedled him into letting me
take her to the Concert, and I don't think
he'll stand for another strike. I thought you

and your influence could help me — if you would."

"Does n't it seem to you as if you were acting rather hoggishly?" I answered gravely. "Why can't you let the Kid have her? She 'll be his guest, and you know how much he likes her?"

"That 's not the point. The Kid has been fresh to me, and I propose to teach him a lesson. Won't hurt him a bit! Why, he had the nerve the other day to say that he did not believe I was one, two, three with Miss Archlen. Said he knew her very well, and never even heard her speak of me. Said it in his mean little way too, and walked off laughing and holding his young head in the air as if he were the whole thing. Hoggish? Not! It 's time he knew something. If you won't join in the good work, all right — I 'll do it myself." And he tossed back his wavy hair with a look of supreme self-confidence.

I had become black in the face from this harangue. Verily, the Freshman was learning human nature, and was already feeling the proximity of sophomore year. When I could trust myself to speak, I said, "Maybe you are right, Morley. I'll see what I can do for you," and Morley thanked me and strolled away.

I fixed it with the Freshman, and Morley chuckled gleefully. After that, he made several other minor engagements. When the Freshman was fixing the box for the ball, Morley was to take Miss Archlen walking. When the Kid and his classmates were fixing our house for our own dance, Morley was to read to Miss Archlen up in the shady nooks of the second gorge. Meanwhile, in an owlish conference held by the Kid and me, it was decided that at those times I should take care of Miss Edith Archlen. In every detail our plan was complete. The enemy's discomfiture and defeat were certain, and we breathed easily while awaiting developments.

At last the first of the war clouds crept down from the north. On the morning of the day our guests were all expected to arrive, the Freshman handed me Miss Archlen's card. At the break-fast-table I casually mentioned to Morley that I was going to have Miss Archlen's elder sister as my guest. All Morley said, was, "Did n't know she had a sister; pass me the bread, please?"

Danger number one was over, and I knew the fuse would be longer burning than I had dared to hope.

There was the usual flurry and bustle as the noon train rolled in with its cargo of peaches and cream and dried apples. The girls were hailed with the usual shouts of joy, and the chaperons with the usual exaggerated politenesses. In the rush, Morley failed to meet the elder Miss Archlen, and it was not until luncheon that he had that pleasure. Even then all he said to me in an aside was, "Jove, but she's pretty."

She was. I am not going to describe her, but she was undeniably a beautiful girl with a great deal of wit and, best of all, a keen sense of humor. If I had n't known some one else who had sailed for Europe with my sister, this story might have been different. To my mind, she was infinitely superior to her sister in looks, and in most other ways, and I think Morley thought so too, but his blood was up, and all his batteries of fascination were brought to bear upon her younger sister.

By dinner-time his face wore a look of doubt. All the afternoon he had been hearing the two girls called Miss Archlen and Miss Edith Archlen, and I think he smelled a rat. That evening he had to go to a Phi Beta Kappa initiation, and when he returned every one was asleep, so that the day was passed in quiet. That the bombardment and mine explosion would occur the next morning, I did not doubt. That the enemy would be overthrown, I was sure. That he would accept defeat gracefully, and in the spirit in which it was given, I was not.

And I was right.

The morning of Tuesday, June 17, 1890, dawned bright and clear. For modern warfare the day was perfect. A cloudless sky and a gentle wind heartened both forces. The Buffalo

Royal Volunteers occupied the most advantageous position, being ensconced in a large leather chair fortified by pillows. She was well reinforced by a brigade of the Buffalo Light Blue Infantry, and two companies of the 94th and 90th N. G. I. Reserves, who had taken up positions in a clump of chairs slightly in the rear and on the left flank. The opposing forces, consisting of a brigade of Morley's Own, occupied higher ground about three feet south. He was on a window-seat.

The first gun was fired at exactly 9.43 A. M. Morley asked Miss Edith Archlen if she remembered two years ago this summer. Miss Edith Archlen looked over her pillows and sighed, and said yes. Morley's Own slid a foot and a half nearer, and they began to reminisce.

Morley said, "Do you remember the old south pier, and how we used to walk over there at sunset and watch the waves come booming in?"

"As if it were yesterday," sighed Miss Edith, looking out the corner of her eye to see what the Freshman was doing.

"I wonder if the ivy we planted still grows?" meditated the enemy.

"We planted it together," said Miss Edith; "it ought to."

"They were happy times," said Morley, and looked as if he were thinking about them.

"They were for me," said Miss Edith, frankly; "and I never tasted such goods things to eat in all my life."

Morley looked a little hurt, and the Reserves stuffed handkerchiefs into their mouths.

"I wonder if we shall ever go sword-fishing again! I'm afraid that I shall have to wait a long time before I can stand at the rail of a two-master and look across a limitless, tossing, rolling ocean. Things change when a man leaves college," hazarded Morley.

"You were sick that day," mused Miss Edith.

"Er — yes," said Morley.

Silence. Then a shriek of delight from the Buffalo Light Blue Infantry, who had discovered in the visitors' book the name of a girl she knew. The 90th N. G. I. scratched a match.

"Do you remember the old South Light?" asked Miss Edith.

"And the periwinkle rocks below it?"

"And the grizzled old lightkeeper I used to sketch?"

"And the lightkeeper's little daughter?"

"Yes; wasn't she pretty? Those roguish eyes and the sweetest rosebud mouth!"

"I never thought so," said Morley.

"No? She told me you tried one afternoon."

"I never did," said he, indignantly, and the clump of chairs chuckled.

More silence, while Morley's indignation ebbed, and Miss Edith looked pensive, then —

"I — do you want to know why I never did — Edith?"

"My name is Archlen."

"I know; but I can't call you Archlen. No one ever calls a girl by her last name that way."

"You know what I meant."

"Once you let me call you Edith," whispered Morley.

The reinforcements fixed bayonets, but the ranks of the Buffalo Royal Volunteers, beyond a slight disorder, held fast, and no command was given.

"That was five years ago," said Miss Edith Archlen.

"What difference does that make?"

"Five years."

"And you don't want me to now?"

"I hardly think it best. What difference does it make to you? None, and you know it. I have grown older, Mr. Morley, and I know more than I once did."

"And you think I don't care, O 'sage'?"

With Morley, sarcasm was danger. We tightened our cartridge-belts.

"I know you don't."

"You know it," echoed the enemy, scornfully. "How full of wisdom you have become! You *know* it! When I — ever since I heard you were coming — have been plotting, planning, and scheming to see something of you. Why, if I don't care, should I have twelve dances with you at the Senior? Why should I trouble my-self to take you to the Concert? Why did I beg for your company on the boat ride, and why have I made numberless minor engage ments with you?" Morley's Own were charg-ing, and I held my breath for the destruction that was sure to follow.

There was a deathly stillness, then Miss Edith Archlen said, "What do you mean? I have not a single dance on my card with you. I am going to the Concert with the man that asked me here. I am going to the boat ride with him. On Wednesday evening, I am going to the Masque with him. He has made no engagements for me with you, because — humiliating as it is, sir — you have not asked for them."

"Wha-at? You are joking," said Morley. "Oh, you are, you know! But I did, I tell you. Has that Kid — ? *Come here, Freshman!*"

The Buffalo Royal Volunteers looked on in wide amazement, and the 94th N. G. I. Reserve wheeled and clattered to the front with muskets

at the charge.   The 90th N. G. I. and the Light
Blue retired from the field to the piazza.

" I am afraid the end is near," said I, solemnly,
for we had decided it best to tell Miss Archlen
all about our plots.

" And I shall be despised," said she.

" Hush ! " I replied, " you probably have saved
the happiness of two people's lives."

" But I don't like to be despised by Mr.
Morley," she observed.

" You won't be," said I, and then, while the
recording angel scratched his chin in perplexity,
I whispered in her ear that Morley had wished
to me last night that he had all those dances
and other engagements with her instead of with
her sister.

It was a bold stroke, but it told, and it was
pretty to see her blush as I hurried her out of
earshot, to save my lie.

.   .   .   .

The Freshman told me afterwards that he
actually felt sorry for Morley when he discovered his suicide.   Of course the Freshman

was sorry for his mistake, and thought when Morley said Miss Archlen that he meant Miss Archlen. If he had known, of course — and so forth; but that only made Morley all the more angry. He insisted that he had been cheated. He ranted around and tore his hair, and wanted things all changed. This the Freshman regretted exceedingly could not be done. He pointed out that it would mix things all up. If he had only known before, it might have been arranged, but —. When Morley asked for a dance, and found Blake had just taken the only one remaining on the card, when he asked if he might not go walking with her the next morning, and remembered that at that time he had promised to go walking with her sister, when he suggested a sail on the following afternoon, and was reminded of his engagement to inspect the second gorge, and when, finally, in desperation he had attacked every flank and tried every loop-hole to no avail, he fell back upon the window-seat and ignominiously surrendered. Then he rose, swore at the Kid, begged Miss Edith's pardon, said he'd been a fool, shook hands with them both, and excused himself.

Then the Freshman told the now thoroughly disorganized Buffalo Royal Volunteers all about it. He told her his fears, his hopes, and other things he felt; and when the elder Miss Archlen and I returned, the strangest thing in the history of any war had happened, for the Buffalo Royal Volunteers had surrendered to her own Reserves.

That night after the ball, Morley poked his head into my room.

" Billy," said he, " you 're a beast."

" Yes?" said I.

" And I 'm a fool," said he.

" Yes," said I.

" Go to blazes," he remarked sweetly, and withdrew grinning.

" Freshman," said I, to the sweetly dreaming boy in bed, " it 's dollars to doughnuts that Kingsland N. Morley is married first," and he was — to the elder Miss Archlen.